Foul Play

Beverly Scudamore

James Lorimer & Company Ltd., Publishers
Toronto

James Lorimer & Company Ltd. acknowledges the support of the Ontario Arts Council. We acknowledge the support of the Government of Canada through the Book Publishing Industry Development Program (BPIDP) for our publishing activities. We acknowledge the support of the Canada Council for the Arts for our publishing program. We acknowledge the support of the Government of Ontario through the Ontario Media Development Corporation's Ontario Book Initiative.

Cover illustration: Greg Ruhl

The Canada Council for the Arts | Le Conseil des Arts du Canada

ONTARIO ARTS COUNCIL
CONSEIL DES ARTS DE L'ONTARIO

National Library of Canada Cataloguing in Publication Data

Scudamore, Beverly
    Foul play / Beverly Scudamore.

(Sports stories ; 79)
ISBN 1-55028-875-X (bound)   ISBN 1-55028-874-1 (pbk.)

I. Title. II. Series: Sports stories (Toronto, Ont.); 79.

PS8587.C82F68 2005   jC813'.54   C2005-900230-1

James Lorimer & Company Ltd., Publishers
35 Britain Street
Toronto, Ontario
M5A 1R7
www.lorimer.ca

Distributed in the United States by:
Orca Book Publishers
P.O. Box 468
Custer, WA USA
98240-0468

Printed and bound in Canada.

Contents

For Mom and Dad

1

A Brilliant Tackle

Trapped!

Alison Andrews had me marked. Her feet dug at the soccer ball as she tried to steal it away. I needed help. Fast!

Kristi Simpson darted up on the right and called to me. "Remy, I'm open!" She zigged left, then circled back. I tried to aim the ball, but Alison pounced like a wildcat. My only hope was to break out, then make a quick pass.

"Now!" Kristi called, her braces glinting in the sun.

Before I could react, Alison tackled me from the side, her foot sliding under mine as she poked the ball away. Flying through the air, I landed face first, eating grass. I stayed down, waiting for the whistle. A strange quiet surrounded me. I realized both teams were still running. I scrambled to my feet in time to see Alison power the ball to her teammate. The girl drove a high ball just beyond our goalkeeper's fingers and into the net. The red team took the lead: 2–1.

"That was a penalty!" I yelled, but the ref, a teenage girl, ignored me.

I glanced over at our coach, Jenn Rentola, for support, but she shook her head. Did no one else see?

From the sidelines, I heard my Dad's deep voice. "Remy!" Noting the deep furrows creasing his brow, I got the message:

settle down. My parents were sitting on lawn chairs under a large sun umbrella at their usual spot by the midfield line.

The U13 recreation soccer league, made up of twelve-and-thirteen-year-old girls, plays on Friday nights at six o'clock, just as the sun is beginning to sink into the west, angling its blinding rays into the crowd's eyes. The team benches are located on the opposite side of the field to protect our ears from the occasional loudmouthed spectator.

Our teams don't have names, just colours. I play forward, a striker, on the "blue" team, and I wear number 6. Our team is sponsored by Benny's Bagels, a small bakery in downtown Glendale. Sometimes the owner, Benny, brings fresh, warm bagels out to the game. Scrummy! His daughter, Marie, plays defence on our team, and she has awesome spirit. No matter how badly we play, Marie always has something good to say.

Our chief opposition, the red team, sponsored by Comet Chemicals, is first place in the league. We are a close second. Here's the thing: when our team plays full strength, we can beat the red team. Too often we play shorthanded, and in the melting heat we start collapsing before the end of the half.

At least tonight we had one substitute player. We could still win this game.

Both sides headed to centre field for the kickoff. Alison ran alongside me, tucking loose strands of her strawberry-blonde hair back into a ponytail. "Are you okay, Remy?"

Wiping dirt off my elbows, I glared into her frosty, blue eyes. "You mean, after you tripped me?"

"That was a brilliant tackle," she replied. "I only touched the ball."

"Then why'd I fall?"

"'Cause you lost your balance. You were watching Kristi instead of the ball."

"Was not," I growled, walking off to take my position.

There was a short delay when a ball from a nearby game rolled onto our field. I stepped over to talk to my best friend, Nina Patel, who was lined up next to me. Nina was born in India. Her parents immigrated to Canada when she was four years old. She has a tiny turned-up nose, wide-set brown eyes, and silky black hair that falls neatly down her back. Her delicate looks fool a lot of people. Nina is the top striker on our team. Her long, slender legs never seem to tire, and she's a fast sprinter. She knows she's good, but she doesn't brag about it like some people I know.

"Poor Remy! Nice face plant," Nina teased, propping her arm on my shoulder. "You've got dirt on your cheek."

I wiped my face with my sweaty arm. "Better?"

She laughed. "Now you've smeared it across your face."

I glowered at Alison who had taken her position deep in the field. "She's such a show-off," I said. "Ever since she went to that soccer camp in England last summer, she thinks she's a pro. Have you noticed how she calls soccer 'football' like they do in Europe, and what's with 'brilliant'?"

"That's the British way of saying awesome," Nina said.

"But she's not from England!"

"A month of soccer training did improve her game."

"Well, it didn't help her personality," I countered.

Nina shot me a look. "Wow, you sound angry."

"Yeah, so? I still remember."

"But it happened a long time ago," Nina said. "Maybe if you speak to her. I mean … what if she had a good reason?"

"Friends don't treat each other that way," I said.

"Lighten up," Nina said, making a goofy face. "Don't let her get to you. Haven't you heard the expression 'don't get mad, get even?'"

My eyes widened with interest. "What do you have in mind?"

"We are down by one goal, and there are only three minutes left in the game. Let's tie it up."

Although I'm not sure Nina understood the meaning of get even, she did make a good point. We needed to tie the game — and quickly.

The red team moved a midfielder back to play defence, making it difficult for us to advance on their net. One of their players had the ball, and she was dribbling up the wing into our territory. Time was running out.

"Heads up!" Jenn called from the bench. "Don't let her get by!"

Marie responded by intercepting the ball and slamming a World Cup kick, straight upfield to our midfielder, Shani Kenyatta. Shani ran like crazy toward the net.

"Twenty seconds!" Jenn called. "Kick it, Shani!"

She hesitated, trying to set up the kick. Meanwhile, behind her, two red players were closing in.

"Now!" Jenn called.

Shani booted the ball high at the goal. We watched helplessly as it soared up, up, and over the crossbar. Cries of joy rang out from the red team. Shani dropped her head into her hands and let out a loud groan.

The ref blew the whistle signalling the end of the game.

Marie ran over to Shani. "Nice try!" she said. "You were close."

Shani rolled her eyes. "Yeah, if my target was a bird."

"Don't feel bad," I said. "I've done the same thing."

We trudged back to centre field for the handshake.

"Good game," Jenn said, patting our backs. "I heard lots of communication on the field, just like we practised."

Nina got in line behind me. "Did you bring money?"

"Nope," I said, "but my parents did."

A few minutes later, I found Mom and Dad talking to Alison's mom. Their lawn chairs were folded and tucked under their arms.

"Good game," Mom said, ruffling my hair.

Dad reached for his wallet. He knew the routine. As he handed me the cash, he whispered, "Fetch me one, too."

Mom heard, and she replied with a withering stare, "Roger O'Sullivan …"

"Gelato is a healthy choice," he argued, weakly.

"Remember the doctor's instructions," she warned.

He turned to me and sighed. "Maybe next time."

At the edge of the soccer park stands a little ice cream hut with a bubble roof. At least that's what it looks like from a distance. Up close, the bubbles are actually plastic soccer balls and the sign says "Kicks." It opened this spring and sells forty-one flavours of ice cream. Sweet! The owner and main scooper is Luigi. It's no wonder Luigi is crazy about soccer — his cousin, who lives in Italy, played in a World Cup.

Luigi creates his own chocolate gelato, an Italian ice cream made with milk instead of cream. Luigi doesn't use any old chocolate. He imports smooth Belgian chocolate, the kind that feels like velvet on your tongue. The secret family recipe was handed down through many generations. Luigi adds his own special touch on top of each cone: a soccer gumball. The other forty flavours are a commercial brand. Practically everybody runs to get ice cream after every game.

"Ciao!" Luigi greeted us, as we entered. "What will it be?"

"Gelato!" Nina and I chorused.

While Luigi was scooping, my eyes gazed at the photos on the walls — top men's and women's teams from around the world. Suddenly, a colourful poster caught my attention. It read:

"The First Annual Kicks Soccer Tournament." And below: "For Recreation Players."

My heart sped up. Yes! Normally, the competitive divisions get to play in tournaments. Passing over the details, I arrived at the important part. First place: an all-inclusive day pass to Wacky Water World. Second place: a Kicks cone for each team member.

"Whoo-hoo!" I exclaimed. "This tournament rocks!"

"Speaking of rocks," Kristi said, butting in next to me. "Does that include the Slippery Rock climbing wall, Luigi?"

He nodded. "Water slides, the wave pool, the Eel River Ride. Did I forget anything?"

"Awesome!" Marie shouted, breaking into a dance.

"The tournament is on Saturday, June 26th," Nina observed. "That's in three weeks — the first day of summer break."

My mouth watered as Luigi handed me the cone. My body was still pumping out heat like a furnace. The frozen gelato melted as it hit my mouth and slipped smoothly down my throat. I picked the soccer gumball off the top, setting it aside on a napkin for later.

Josh Elliot, a guy in my class, came to the door wearing in-line skates. He bent over to remove them.

"Come as you are!" Luigi called, waving him in. "The floor is cement. You can't hurt it."

Josh smoothed his wavy, brown hair out of his eyes. "Really? Hey, I like this place."

Nina called to him, "Why are you here?"

"My sister's playing," he replied, walking up to the ice cream counter.

"Want to see something amazing?" I directed him to the poster. "Check out the prizes."

Josh didn't look impressed. "The tournament is the same day as the Skate Jam. You both promised you'd come."

Nina and I exchanged glances.

"We just found out about the tournament," I explained. "But we'll try to watch part of the Skate Jam."

"You won't be sorry," he said. "There's going to be amazing demonstrations and crazy contests. Admission is only a loonie. We're raising funds for new ramps and rails and …" he paused. "There's more. It's really big."

"A pro's coming?" Nina guessed.

"Nope," Josh said, "but get this — a major company is going to introduce a new sport drink called X-Juice at our event. How cool is that? A drink made exclusively for skaters!"

Just then, Alison and her teammate, Emily, entered. They walked up to the poster. "A day at Wacky Water World!" Alison exclaimed. "We are most definitely going to win."

The two girls high-fived each other.

"Got to go," I said, rolling my eyes. "My parents are waiting."

Popping the soccer gumball into my mouth, I headed out the door.

2

Grossology

Summer break was fast approaching. In two weeks, Pearson Elementary would close its doors. Grade 7 would be over, and I could finally escape the loser who sits behind me. His name is Lucas Baxter. The guy calls himself a scientist. Normally, I think science is cool. I mean, where would we be without calculators and computers, cures for diseases, cell phones … chocolate bars?

But Lucas is different. He studies a yucky, twisted science that I call Grossology.

Case in point: at the beginning of the year, Lucas brought glass microscope slides to school, asking students with colds for donations. The guy claimed that he could tell if a person should see a doctor based on the colour and texture of their nasal samples. Okay, that's disgusting! And it gets worse. Our teacher, Mr. Jackson, overheard me calling him Mucous Lucas.

"Miss O'Sullivan," he said, pointing at me, "May I have a word with you in the hall?"

Mr. Jackson gave me a detention and a long talk about respecting others' differences. When I tried to explain that I had caught Lucas removing a used tissue from the trash can, the teacher didn't flinch. He called Lucas's warped behaviour *gifted*. Excuse me? Who would want that sort of gift?

Then Lucas had become obsessed with earthworms. Kevin told me he was growing them in his desk.

"I've got him now," I laughed to myself.

When I took this slimy knowledge to Mr. Jackson and begged him to let me change desks, it backfired in my face. He warned *me* to stop picking on Lucas.

But now Mr. Jackson stood before the class, dressed in a suit and tie. "Bring out your math texts," he instructed. "Turn to page 345 and read the section called Constructing Parallel Lines. Then complete the exercises that follow."

I was busy reading when Lucas tapped me on the back. "Did you know that worms are 82 percent protein? That is more protein than chicken or beef. Pretty amazing, eh?"

I glowered at him. "Like, why should I care?"

"Worms are an important food source for some people," he explained.

"Not for me," I replied, stone-faced. Turning back to my desk, I brought out a ruler and compass, then got down to work drawing parallel lines.

"Remy!" His fingers thumped on my back. "There is something else you might find interesting."

"As long as it's not about worms," I warned.

"Oh … okay, forget it," he said.

Here's the tragedy. Lucas is cute. He's got tan skin, milk chocolate brown eyes (did I mention I love chocolate?), and long, dark bangs that are forever falling into his eyes. He could be a major hottie, if only …

A crazy idea came to me. Maybe I could teach him to be cool.

He knocked on my shoulder. "Did you know the longest earthworm on record is two metres long? That's as tall as Mr. Jackson."

Scrap that idea, I told myself. There is no hope.

On the way outside for lunch break, I stopped by the washroom, mostly to check my hair. A few weeks ago, I visited the hairdresser, and got my long brown hair cut in layers, just like a teen model I had admired in a magazine. That girl's layers fell straight and funky. My layers flip up on one side of my head, and under on the other. The worst part — I paid for the cut with my own money.

When my eyes met the mirror, horror struck. My hair was not the problem. A new zit had popped up on my chin, and it stuck out like a raspberry. Why hadn't I noticed it before? I would have applied concealer. Lately, pimples blossom on my oily skin.

I was locking the stall door when the main washroom door flew open. Familiar voices approached: Alison and Emily, from the other grade 7 class across the hall.

"I've got to get this chocolate milk out of my shirt before my mom sees it," Alison said, sounding close to tears. "She's in an awful mood these days. She flips out over nothing."

Tap water began to slosh loudly in the sink, making their conversation difficult to hear, but I still managed.

"Use the soap from the dispenser," Emily suggested. "It's really strong. It got ketchup out of my shorts the other day."

"Did the coach call you about the tournament?" Alison asked.

"Yep," Emily replied. "I can't wait. We have a good chance of winning. Our only real competition is the blue team. When they have a full team, they're tough to beat."

"We'll win," Alison said, in a smug tone. "Guaranteed."

"How can you be so confident?" Emily said.

"Trust me. I have a plan."

My heart started to drum. I held my breath so I could catch every word, but Alison changed the subject.

"The stain's almost gone. Can you grab me some paper towels? I'm soaking wet."

"What kind of plan?" Emily insisted.

Yeah, spit it out, I thought, leaning forward.

More girls arrived, chatting and laughing, drowning out Alison's voice. Straining to hear, I pressed my ear against the stall. But the lock on the door was defective! Next thing I knew, I was falling, grabbing at air.

Emily jumped out of my way as I flew past her. "What the …?"

Alison fixed her frosty glare upon me. "Were you eavesdropping?"

"For your information, I was going to the washroom," I said, trying to compose myself. "Not that it's any of your business."

"You took a long time," Emily said.

I dug my fists into my hips. "Do you mind respecting my privacy?"

Emily turned to Alison. "Let's go outside where it's warm. The sun will dry your shirt."

After they left, Nina called through the door. "Remy, are you going to spend the entire lunch break in the washroom?"

"Coming," I replied.

"Well, hurry. I spotted a hummingbird in the butterfly garden."

I followed Nina to the side of the school, past the wooden sign that reads, "Quiet: butterfly zone." For the past two years, each grade has cared for a different section of the butterfly garden. The students planted bushes and flowers that share one thing in common: their colours and aromas attract butterflies. In the centre of the garden is a large pictorial chart that identifies different local species of butterflies.

The garden was our principal's idea. She read a bunch of studies that showed if students get a chance to relax during the day, there are fewer behaviour problems at school.

Nina and I hurried along the wood chip path. "It's gone!" she cried. "It looked like a little jewel and it was hovering in a flower." Grabbing onto my arm, she blurted, "News flash! Did you know that besides nectar, hummingbirds eat tiny insects hiding in the blossoms?"

Interesting, but I had other things on my mind. "Come sit," I said, leading her to a bench beside a patch of milkweed.

"I've got something to tell you," I said, in a hushed tone. "For your ears only."

Nina's eyes widened.

"It's about the soccer tournament," I went on. "Alison is plotting against our team."

Her tiny nose wrinkled. "You're kidding, right?"

I slowly shook my head. "I overheard her in the washroom just now."

She studied my face. "What's she going to do?"

"I'm not sure," I said. "Alison and Emily stopped talking when they realized I was in the room."

Nina frowned. "That doesn't sound like Alison."

"Maybe not the old Alison," I said, "but she's changed. Haven't you noticed? I can't believe I used to be her friend."

"Maybe she's upset about her parents," Nina noted. "and maybe it's affecting her. We've never been close friends, so I wouldn't know for sure."

"My parents fight," I argued, "but I don't take it out on my friends."

Nina leaned forward. "You know that Mr. and Mrs. Andrews are separated, right?"

"Huh? Are you serious?" I slumped down on the bench. For a moment, I felt sorry for Alison. I even began to wonder: is it possible? Could her parents' problems explain why she had acted so rotten to me?

"Even so …" I said, still feeling unsure, "that doesn't change things."

"Think about it," Nina said, flipping her long hair behind her back. "How could Alison sabotage a soccer game? She can't mess with the ball when both teams use it. And she can't get to our shoes and uniforms. Each girl is in charge of her own equipment."

Nina did have a point.

"Still," I insisted, "she's up to something."

"Shhh …" Nina grabbed my hand. "Over there in the red clover!"

"Hmmm … yellow with black stripes, and a dash of brilliant blue on its wing tips." I thought for a moment, then turned to Nina. "I give up."

Silently, we crept toward the butterfly. Up close, we could see its long proboscis sipping nectar from the clover blossoms. Just then, the bell rang. We hurried to consult the chart.

Nina found our butterfly quickly. "Canadian Tiger Swallowtail," she said.

"Know something?" I said, as we turned to leave. "The butterfly garden doesn't work. We wasted the entire recess sitting here, and I'm not feeling calm. Alison is up to something. I'm going to find out what she's planning and stop her."

3

Defying Gravity

At first, Josh didn't notice us since he was concentrating on a new move. Nina and I leaned against the chain-link fence, watching him approach a rail. He crouched low, then smacked the tail of his skateboard down with his back foot and ollied high, landing on the rail. Balancing on the thin bar, he began to nose-grind down. His arms started to flail. His board shifted. Suddenly, he lost his balance and slammed onto the cement. We watched him attempt the same move three times. Each time, he wiped out. Mrs. Elliot sat in the bleachers, her hand cupped over her mouth.

"Having fun?" I called as he was recovering from his latest crash.

"Your mother looks like she's going to have a heart attack," Nina noted.

He skated over. "I'm going to ride that rail if it kills me."

"Maybe it would help if you tightened your laces," Nina suggested. "Your shoes look like they're about to fall off."

Josh shot her a "not cool" look.

"Where'd you learn to ollie so high?" I asked. "The skateboard looks like it's glued to your feet in the air. Isn't that, like, impossible?"

Josh brushed his wavy hair back and smiled. "Skaters defy gravity."

"Whatever," Nina said. "We're not on the moon. What's your secret?"

Before he could answer, we got sidetracked. Another skater, this one with a mop of red hair, dropped into the half-pipe. The skater came burning down the ramp and up the other side. Before he reached the lip, he turned, crouching low to pick up speed, then exploded off the top.

Josh whistled through his fingers. "Big air!"

Nina and I cheered along.

"Skeeter rules around here," Josh acknowledged.

"We know him," Nina said. "He's our soccer coach's boyfriend."

We watched a girl riding a BMX bike drop into the pipe. Next came some old dude on a skateboard. He was wearing Hawaiian shorts with a flowered lei draped around his neck. As he went into a turn, a skater wearing a black muscle shirt cut him off.

Josh winced as the Hawaiian skater took a dive.

I nudged him. "Who is that creep?"

He grimaced. "Razor."

"What kind of name is that?"

"He turns sharp edges with his board. But the name fits on another level: He cuts off skaters like they don't exist, and if anyone gets in his face he slices them with his tongue. Let's just say he doesn't help the skatepark's reputation. It makes me mad, you know, because it was so hard to get city council to support the skaters."

Even though I'm not into boarding, I knew of the local skaters' struggles to get a park. For years they had approached city hall, asking council to provide a safe place in which to practise their sport. Skeeter led the way, gathering petitions, conducting surveys, speaking at council meetings, even getting local business owners to support the skaters. Eventually, the city agreed to build a skatepark. The council members consulted with the skaters to design a decent park. And they did an amazing job. The skatepark has a three-metre half-pipe, an oval bowl that resembles an empty swimming pool, ramps, rails, curbs. A chain-link fence surrounds the park. Skaters can buy a membership or pay two bucks for a day pass. The money goes toward paying a manager who keeps the skaters in line. Get it? In-line.

"Skeeter!" I called. By the stunned look on his face, I could tell he didn't recognize us at first. When his brain clicked, he skated over. "S'up, soccer girls?"

"We came to watch Josh practise," I said.

He propped an elbow on Josh's shoulder. "Hey, man, did you hear about the new sport drink? Wonder if the company is looking to sponsor some young, hot skater?" He touched his finger to his chest and made a sizzling sound. "I could use the extra money."

"Yeah," Josh laughed. "I've seen how many boards you go through."

"Tell me about it," he grumbled, wiping the sweat from his brow.

"Are you coming to soccer practice tonight?" Nina asked, but something distracted Skeeter.

"Whoa!" he exclaimed. "Did you see that? A kid spilled off the curb and slammed down on his arm. The little dude's lucky he's wearing wrist guards." He jumped on his board. "Think I'll check him out. See you two later."

When Skeeter was at a safe distance, Nina turned to me. "What does Jenn see in him? I mean, he's fun, but he doesn't seem like the boyfriend type."

"What is the boyfriend type?" I said, dreamily casting my eyes upward.

"You know … romantic."

I laughed. "Nina, you watch too much TV. Come on. Let's go watch Josh wipe out again."

* * *

Coming home is not easy anymore — or safe.

Creeping up to the door, I reached out, slowly twisting the handle. The hinge creaked. My body tensed. He came running, gaining speed as he approached. Tossing my backpack on the floor, I braced myself. Wham! A full body slam. This time I managed to stay on my feet.

"Bad dog!" I cried. "That's no way to answer the door."

Tucker wasn't listening. He was a blur of fur and claws as he jumped and spun in circles.

"Mom!"

No answer.

"Mom!" I yelled louder. "When is Tucker going to obedience school? He can't be flattening people at the door. He's going to hurt someone one day."

Still no answer. I ran to the desk to check Mom's real estate appointment book. She was showing a house at four o'clock. That meant she wouldn't be home for a while.

Tucker is my eight-month-old Springer Spaniel. Although he is still a puppy, he is almost full-grown. When he jumps on his hind legs, his paws reach my shoulders. And he packs the power of a freight train.

For years, I begged my parents to let me have a dog. I told them, "Since I am an only child, I deserve the company of a pet."

Although my parents liked dogs, they felt it wouldn't be fair to keep one cooped up in an empty house while they were at work and I was at school. Then, in grade 7 — surprise! They sat me down for a serious dog talk. Naturally, I promised to be responsible for a puppy, walking it before and after school, feeding and grooming it — the whole deal. A few weeks later, when I picked up the cute little bundle of brown-and-white fur, I had no idea that I had chosen the monster of the litter.

Kneeling on the rug, I gave Tucker a hug. "Good boy. Remy's best puppy in the whole world." I puckered up. "Kisses." Tucker didn't lick. He gnawed on my wrist.

Yanking my arm free, I said, "Time to go outside."

Walking through the living room, I felt something wet on my sock. Staring down, I discovered a round, dark mark on the carpet. Tucker's tail slipped between his legs. He slunk off under the dinner table. Muttering, I went to the kitchen and grabbed a roll of paper towels. As I dutifully cleaned up the "accident," Tucker began to bark playfully.

"It's not funny," I barked back.

All of a sudden, he came bounding out from under the table, grabbed the roll of paper towels and ran off.

"Get back here!" I yelled, sprinting after him. He didn't listen. He ran in circles, deking me out whenever I got close.

"Fine!" I said, throwing my arms up. "Have it your way!" I stormed upstairs and shut myself in my bedroom. Tucker sat outside my door, whimpering.

"Go away!"

A little later, I heard Mom walk in the door. "Down! You put a run in my nylons."

"Hi, Mom," I called, jogging down the stairs.

"Hi, Remy. How was your …" her voice broke off. "What on earth?"

I found Mom standing in the doorway. Her lips were pursed as she gazed into the living room. It looked like winter had arrived early. The rug was covered in snow. Tucker had shredded the roll of paper towels into tiny bits. He looked pleased with himself. Mom looked like she was going to pop a vein.

Mindful of our serious "dog talk," the one where I promised to be responsible, I said, "Don't worry, I'll vacuum up the mess."

"That much paper will clog the hose," Mom warned.

I thought for a moment, then ran outside to fetch a rake.

As I raked the carpet, Tucker grabbed onto the metal prongs, playing tug-of-war. I distracted him with doggy bones. When the rug was finally clean, he sat next to me, resting his head on my lap, staring up at me with his big, brown eyes. I buried my head in his soft fur.

"Are you ever going to learn?" I said, planting a kiss on his head.

He took my hand in his mouth and began to chew.

4

Skeeter Says ...

Jenn Rentola is a soccer nut. She's on the field most days, either playing on the city league or high school soccer. She's a grade 12 student and next year she will attend university on a soccer scholarship. Despite her busy schedule, she still finds time to coach our team. Having a teenager for a soccer coach is very cool. Let's just say I never know what's going to happen at practice, especially when her boyfriend shows up to help.

Glendale must have a lot of soccer nuts because Jenn could not find a free pitch for our Wednesday evening practices. Instead, she settled for a grassy field in Cedar Glen Park. Near the entrance is the playground equipment — tires that spin, swings, slides, climbers. To the left is a baseball diamond. Farther back are the picnic tables and washrooms. A short walk along the nature trail leads to the cedar forest and a shallow creek. The best thing about Cedar Glen Park is it's in my neighbourhood. This makes my parents happy, since they don't have to drive me to practice. Mom is a real estate agent, and Dad is a salesman for the Tasty Treats company, so they both spend too much time in their cars.

Our practice field is located at the edge of the cedar forest. It's obvious the area isn't intended for soccer since the grass is cut long, weeds stretch up to the sun, and there are no nets. But we don't mind. It's our special place.

Five minutes before practice, Jenn rode up on her bike, wearing a pink tank top and soccer shorts. While she fought with the kickstand, I walked up. "Hey, Jenn, did you sign us up for the tournament? It's in less than two weeks."

"Just a sec," she said. Snapping the kickstand into place, she propped up her bike, then stood back and watched it fall to the ground. She left it there. Next, she tucked her short, dark hair into a ponytail. Most of it fell out, leaving behind a puppy tail. Finally, she turned to me. "Before we enter, I need to make sure we can form a team. The players don't seem very dedicated."

Jenn gazed over at the field, counting girls. "Only six tonight," she sighed. "The only way this team can improve is if every player shows up."

At six o'clock, Skeeter pulled up in a white van and began unloading the soccer equipment from the back. He looked dressed to skate, wearing a blue hoodie with the Freestyle logo and baggy shorts that fell below his knees.

Jenn waited a few more minutes hoping more players would arrive. When no one else showed up, she blew the whistle and waved us over. "Let's warm up."

"Boring," Kristi said, juggling a ball with her knees.

"Loosening up your muscles helps prevent injury," Jenn said, "and you play better."

We gathered in a semicircle around Jenn while she took us through the stretches. "Standing on one foot, bring the other off the ground and slowly circle your ankle … now the other ankle. Good work. Now, keeping good balance, bring one leg up behind you."

"We look like a flock of flamingos," Shani laughed, toppling over.

Unknown to Jenn, Skeeter was standing behind her, mimicking her. When Jenn finally clued in, she grabbed his hand and pulled him forward.

"Think you can do a better job? Huh, huh?"

Skeeter eagerly nodded his mop of hair. "I was hoping you'd ask." Disappearing to his van, he produced a skateboard.

Jenn thought again. "Forget it, Skeet, the warm up is important. It must be done properly."

"Ready, girls? Let's kick up the action." He grinned, wickedly. "We're going to play Skeeter Says. F.Y.I. that is Simon Says, skater style."

Jenn winked at us. "I have a better idea for a warm up. It's called Catch Skeeter. Okay, skater boy, let's see you deke out six of my best players."

"No thanks," he said, sitting cross-legged on the ground. "Running is not my thing."

Jenn patted him on the back. "Cardio training is good for you. I'll even give you a thirty-second head start."

He didn't budge.

"Twelve … eleven … ten …"

"Boyfriend abuse," he muttered, slowly jogging off.

Jenn laughed. "We'll make a soccer player out of you yet."

In less than ten seconds, Kristi nabbed him by the shirt. The guy was puffing and panting for air. When the rest of the team caught up, we hauled him to the ground. Jenn blew the whistle.

"Back off, girls," she ordered. "I'm the only one allowed to tackle Skeeter."

Then Jenn waved us back to her. "This week we're going to concentrate on dribbling. I'm going to start with an easy relay — dribbling straight up the field and back. That way I can watch your technique. Remember, use good ball control and work at increasing your speed."

We lined up, three girls on each side. Marie dribbled up the field. She passed off to me, and I started back, unsteadily. Dribbling is my weak area.

When I got to the far end, Jenn pulled me aside. "Remy, use both feet when you dribble."

"But I dribble best with my right foot," I said. "My left foot is klutzy."

"Everyone has a strong side," Jenn said. "With practice, your other foot will come along."

"But, it's my style," I insisted, not wanting to change.

"Two feet will allow you to move faster," she insisted, "and to fake out the other team."

To be honest, I was glad when the dribbling drills were over. Dribbling with two feet gives me a headache.

With twenty minutes left in the practice, Jenn called a game of three-on-three.

Sam, our goalkeeper, took her position between two orange cones that represented the net.

Jenn waved Skeeter over. "We need you in goal."

He shook his head. "Why would I stand there, letting those maniacs kick the ball at me?"

"Please," Jenn said, tilting her head. "For me."

Skeeter must have been under a powerful love spell. He couldn't say no.

Jenn placed the ball at the imaginary centre mark, and waited for us to take our positions.

"Playing short-handed gives you a chance to try different positions," she said. "Plus you'll get an awesome workout."

"Finally, a chance to play forward!" Marie exclaimed.

Before I headed onto the field, I took a long drink from my water bottle. Even in the early evening, the sun still sent down hot rays, zapping the moisture from my body.

Marie, Nina, and I made up one team with Sam playing in goal. Kristi, Shani, and Jenn formed the other team. Skeeter sat in their goal, pulling weeds.

Jenn whistled to signal the start of the game. Nina kicked the ball to Marie, who started running straight down the middle. Kristi charged at her, trying to poke the ball away with her foot.

"Pass!" Jenn called. Although Jenn was playing on the opposite side, she was still the coach.

Marie ignored the advice. Kristi ran at her again, this time making a neat tackle and stealing the ball.

Jenn blew the whistle to stop the play. "Marie," she called, "why didn't you pass the ball?"

She gave a sheepish look. "On defence, I don't get a chance to score. I wanted to experience the feeling — just once."

Jenn was cool. She laughed. "Keep playing."

Kristi aimed the ball at Shani, but she misjudged and it soared over Shani's head, rolling out of bounds. I ran to take the throw-in. Standing outside the touchline, I held the ball overhead and gave Marie an eye signal. When I threw it, she trapped the ball with her thigh, then turned and sped toward the goal.

"Move up the field," Jenn called to me. "Marie needs help."

Before I could respond, Marie closed in on the net. She drew her leg back, then followed through with a solid kick. Shani ran in front of the net, blocking the ball with her shoulder, deflecting it off to the wing. Nina sprinted after the loose ball. She took a weird sidestep, followed by a weak kick. Marie ran forward and nabbed the ball. From an angle, she drilled it low and hard at Skeeter. With a yelp, he jumped out of the way.

"I scored!" Marie cried, jumping in the air.

"No fair!" Skeeter protested. "She aimed at me."

Jenn walked over to Marie and gently yanked her ponytail. "Now that you've got the scoring thing out of your system, how about we play like a team?"

"Sure thing," Marie said, beaming. "I'm cured."

When I turned around, I noticed Nina sitting on the field.

"Hey, slacker," I called, walking over. "Get up!"

She didn't answer. As I stepped closer, I could see tears in her eyes.

"What's wrong?" I asked, bending over her.

"I ... I can't get up," she said, her voice breaking. "I stepped in a hole and twisted my ankle."

Sure enough, a few metres away I discovered a fresh divot in the ground.

By this time, Jenn had figured out something was wrong and jogged over to us. When she saw Nina holding her ankle, she called, "Skeet, come quickly."

The team gathered around Nina. But I had to check something out.

Checking the ground, I discovered more divots — six in one corner of the field alone. The ground looked like Swiss cheese. A disturbing thought popped into my mind. The holes in the field. Could Alison have ...? No, even she wouldn't sink that low.

5

Curse of the Tasty Treats

Skeeter kneeled on the grass next to Nina. "May I take a look? First aid was part of my lifeguard training."

She pulled off her socks and shin pads. "Don't touch," she warned.

"The area is swelling," he noted. "Amazing how the body makes its own cast."

"I can't move my foot," Nina groaned. "It hurts so much."

"You're going to end up with a colourful bruise," he said, pointing to a spot that was rapidly turning red and puffy. "My guess is you've sprained your ankle."

"Jenn," he said, "I think you should phone Nina's parents. Ask them to come right away."

Jenn grabbed a cell phone from the leather pouch on her bike and dialled the Patels' number.

Skeeter gave Nina a reassuring smile. "You need to go to the hospital for X-rays to make sure there are no broken bones."

He turned to me. "May I use your lap to elevate her foot?"

"Sure," I said, sitting down directly in front of Nina.

Gently, he lifted Nina's leg to rest on me. "That's all I can do," he said, leaning back on his hands. "Now, we wait for your parents."

Jenn instructed the others to search for and fill in any holes on the field. "I feel awful," she said, hanging her head. "I should have inspected the field before the practice."

"Hey, it was an accident," Skeeter said, standing up to hug her.

"Was it? Those holes looked awfully suspicious," I said. But no one listened to me.

Mr. and Mrs. Patel drove up a few minutes later, with Nina's younger sister, Sita, peering out from the back seat. Skeeter and Jenn assisted Nina to the car, and they spoke briefly with the Patels.

"Phone me when you get back from the hospital," I called to Nina as they drove off.

After Nina's accident, Jenn was too upset to carry on with the game, so we hung out under a tree and talked about stuff. At seven, Dad arrived with Tucker to walk me home. Tucker jumped on everyone, his enthusiastic greeting making the girls scatter, laughing.

"Dad," I said, embarrassed. "I'm old enough to walk home alone."

He pointed to his bulging stomach. "I need the exercise."

Lately, he's been trying to walk more often. So this gives him a convenient excuse to escort me. Geez, I was practically in grade 8.

On the way home, my stomach growled. "What's for dinner?"

"Chicken and broccoli in a cheese sauce. Moist, tender, and, oh so cheesy." Good grief! Dad was sounding like a TV commercial. "Dinner was delicious," he rambled on. "A masterpiece!"

"*Was*? You ate without me?"

"Your mother had to rush off to meet with a new client," he explained. "And I was dropping with hunger. All day long in the van, I didn't sample one Tasty Treat."

"Way to go, Dad," I said, patting him on the back.

Part of Dad's job is to hand out Tasty Treats samples at grocery stores — cream-filled cupcakes, deep-fried sugar donuts, chocolate mud pies. He finds it hard not to sample the goodies himself. Over the years, trying too many samples had pushed Dad's stomach over his belt and into the doctor's office. At his last checkup, the doctor told him that he needed to lose weight and exercise more. Trouble is, the Tasty Treats habit is hard to kick.

As Tucker pulled us along the sidewalk, Dad said, "You can reheat the casserole, and I would be happy to join you. The first time around, there wasn't enough food on my plate to satisfy a mouse."

I rolled my eyes.

At home, I went straight to the kitchen and popped the casserole in the microwave.

As a cheesy aroma filled the air, Dad appeared, hovering over me. "Mmm … smells good."

"You already ate," I reminded him.

"But … I'm fading away to a shadow."

"Sorry, Dad," I said, dumping the leftovers onto my plate. "There isn't enough for two."

After dinner, I finished my science homework and practised on the piano. Mom still wasn't home.

Sure is a long meeting, I thought. Checking her appointment book, I discovered a familiar name: Elaine Andrews. Huh? She's Alison's mom. Why would she meet with Mom … unless they were selling their home?

I wandered up to my bedroom and put on a CD. While I waited for Nina to call or for Mom to come home, I combed my hair, brushed my teeth, and applied ointment to my zits. Eventually, I grew tired and slipped under my covers. Tucker snuggled with me for a while before deciding to get comfortable by stretching out at an angle across the bed and leaving me a corner, where I curled into a ball.

I chuckled to myself, remembering the breeder's advice about raising puppies. She told us Tucker should sleep in a crate. Puppies need a safe spot where they can't chew wires or make messes. She assured us that dogs think of crates as their cave — a happy place.

Not Tucker. Right from the beginning, he cried, a piercing wail that kept the whole family up at night, not to mention his desperate clawing at the gate. The vet insisted that Tucker would eventually accept the crate, he just needed more time. Before that happened, he ripped apart the metal bars and found a new place to sleep — my bed, where he sleeps like an angel. Actually, I like the company. I just wish he would learn not to hog the bed.

That sound? It was a car door. Mom's home, I thought, slipping on my bathrobe. I hurried down the stairs and opened the garage door.

"Mom," I called, peering into the darkness. "Is Alison moving?" Reaching out, I flicked on the light. A figure standing next to the Tasty Treats van turned.

"Dad?" He wiped the creamy evidence from his lips. I noticed a half-eaten mud pie in his hand.

"I only had one," he said, sheepishly. Reaching into the van, he brought out a sugar donut and held it out to me.

A bribe! My own dad had stooped to this! The donut did look tempting. After all, Dad wasn't the only one suffering from a lack of Tasty Treats.

Standing there, something weird happened. I felt like the parent. A lecture was bursting to escape my lips. Oh, no, I was turning into Mom!

At the last second, I bit my tongue. "No thanks," I said, heading into the house, leaving Dad holding the mud pie.

* * *

The bus stop is a block away from the house. Even at that distance, I could still hear Tucker howling. He made it clear that he didn't like being left alone. When Nina didn't get on the school bus that morning, I got really worried. What if she couldn't play in the tournament? Jenn already doubted we could field enough players. If we lost one more …

At first recess, Nina hobbled in on crutches, her foot wrapped in a tensor bandage.

"Why didn't you call?" I said, running up. "I was worried."

"There was a long lineup in the emergency department," she explained. "I waited two hours to see a doctor, then I got sent for X-rays, and that meant another boring wait. Anyway, nothing is broken. We got home after midnight, so Mom let Sita and me sleep in this morning."

"So … what's wrong with your foot?"

"A sprain," she said, "just like Skeeter said. Let's sit in the butterfly garden. I'm supposed to keep my leg elevated whenever possible to keep the swelling down."

I had planned to play soccer with rest of the grade 7s, but it wouldn't be right to ditch my best friend, so I followed her. When she tried to sit on a bench, one crutch flipped into a bush, and she swung through the air on the other, crashing onto the seat.

"Are you sure those help?" I asked, retrieving her crutch.

She laughed. "Watch, I'll probably sprain my other ankle."

Now that we were alone, I got serious. "How soon can you play soccer?"

"Not for three weeks," she said. "Even then, I have to check with the doctor before I can play."

I skipped a breath. "But you'll miss the tournament. Nina, we need you."

"I'll come and cheer for the team," she offered.

What rotten luck! I was sinking into a foul mood, when Nina grabbed my sleeve. "I finally get what Jenn sees in Skeeter. He acts kind of crazy, but when things turn serious, he's totally in control. I never knew he was a lifeguard. That takes a lot of hard work. And," she said, her eyes going goo-goo, "Did you see how he hugged Jenn? That was so sweet."

"Whatever," I said, pushing her playfully.

Lucas came wandering through the garden, holding a bou-quet of dandelions.

"Nice," I sneered. "Are they for your girlfriend?"

"Would you like them?" he said, holding them out to me.

"As if," I said, leaning away. "For your information, I was kidding."

"Good," he said, brushing his bangs out of his eyes. "So was I."

"Oh, yeah, well I knew that." I tried to look cool, but my red face gave me away.

"Actually," he said, "These dandelions are part of my sci-ence project. Did I tell you I belong to the Science Gladiators?"

"A million times," I said, rolling my eyes.

"Is it fun?" Nina asked, leaning forward.

He nodded enthusiastically. "We get to perform awesome experiments in a real lab. Right now, I'm working on an individual project that will be judged by a group of engineers. The winner — that'll be me — goes to science camp in Montreal for a week."

"What's your project?" Nina asked.

He looked at her, then me. His expression changed. "Actually, it's a secret. I don't want the competition to steal my idea."

"We won't tell," Nina said. "Right, Remy?"

I folded my arms. "If it involves worms, I don't want to hear."

Lucas smiled. "Good, I don't want to tell anyway." He held

out a couple of dandelions. "Sample these and tell me if you like the taste."

I pushed his hand away. "Get real!"

"They're pesticide free," Lucas insisted. "I picked them on school property and washed them in the water fountain."

"Dandelions are weeds — not food," I informed him. "My dad sprays our lawn to kill them."

"You should talk to your dad," he said. "Explain that dandelions supply pollen and nectar for the bees."

"Butterflies like nectar too," I said. "In fact, they can have mine." Grabbing a weed from his hand, I tossed it into the bushes.

"Actually, Lucas is right," Nina said. "Dandelions are full of vitamins and minerals. They are healthier than most vegetables. My mom rips up the leaves and puts them in salads."

Why was Nina taking Lucas's side? After all, I did sacrifice recess to sit with her. I was glad when the bell rang, at least until we met Emily and Alison entering the school.

"What happened?" Emily said, running up to Nina.

"I sprained my ankle at soccer practice," she said, hobbling along.

Alison was quick to ask, "What about the tournament?"

Nina frowned. "I'm out."

"Too bad," she said. "Your team's sunk without you."

The tone of her voice was too high. The look in her eyes — they were dancing. She couldn't fool me. Alison wasn't sorry. She was pumped.

"Did you …?" The words burst from my lips before I could stop myself.

"Did I what?" Alison demanded. "Why are you looking at me that way?"

"It's nothing," I said, walking away. "Forget it. We're going to be late for class."

6

Playing Shorthanded

Boring!"

Nina put down the remote control. "Cartoons and reruns. There's nothing good on after school." She lay stretched out on the couch with an ice pack on her ankle, complaining. "My foot's going to get frostbite." "My toes itch." "The crutches hurt my armpits."

Mr. Patel arrived home, carrying a box of donuts. "These were left over from yesterday's staff meeting," he said, setting them down in front of us. "Go ahead. Have one."

"They're stale," Nina grumbled.

"Look good to me," I said, selecting a Dutchie. I hadn't eaten junk food in ages.

"Where's the rest of the family?" he asked.

Nina stared straight ahead. "Mom's in her office writing a business report, and Sita is in the basement playing dress-up with a friend."

"Think I'll check on them," he said.

Nina frowned as she observed me picking out the raisins.

"Why not choose a glazed donut?"

"Dutchies taste better."

"They're the same, except glazed donuts don't have raisins."

I took a bite, then showed her the inside. "Cinnamon."

She clicked her tongue, then stared at the TV screen. Boy, was she grouchy.

Usually Nina and I shot baskets in her driveway, or played ping-pong in her basement, or rode our bikes — stuff like that. To pass time, I stared at the wooden elephant carving on the fireplace mantle. My eyes wandered up to the large picture of a Royal Bengal tiger that hung over the fireplace. The tiger looked peaceful lounging in the grass, yet its head was raised, and its mouth agape in a ferocious roar. Nina always says the tiger was yawning.

"Why don't we play on your computer?" I suggested, finally.

"Nah."

"How about a board game?"

"Did you say *bored*?"

As long as Nina was feeling sorry for herself, we'd both be miserable.

I was about to go home when Mrs. Patel walked into the room. "Mrs. Elliot told me that Josh is preparing for a big festival."

"Skate Jam," Nina corrected.

Mrs. Patel removed the ice pack. "Would you girls like to watch?"

Nina shot her mother a look. "You know, I can't …"

"Such a long face," Mrs. Patel said, pulling Nina's chin. "I need a break from my work. Why don't I drive the two of you? Your father can watch Sita and her friend."

She looked at me. "Want to?"

"Yes!" I said, jumping off the chair.

As Nina struggled with her crutches, I ran ahead and grabbed the brass peacock from the floor so she wouldn't knock it over. Like elephants and tigers, peacocks live in India. The tall birds with the showy feathers roam the countryside and city streets. Not only are they pretty, but they also eat snakes — even poisonous ones.

On the way to the skatepark, Mrs. Patel stopped at Tim

Horton's to buy a cup of green tea. At the park, she took her tea and sat with Mrs. Elliot in the bleachers. Nina and I sat on the cement, close to the action.

"Do you see Josh?" I asked, gazing around.

"Nope," she said, "but there's Skeeter ... and look — some girl on in-line skates is coming down the halfpipe. She's good!"

"Hey, isn't that ..."

"Shani!" we both cried.

Nina turned to me. "Did you know she could skate?"

I shook my head. "We only met two months ago when we got placed on the same soccer team."

"She goes to McKenzie Street School," Nina said. "That's why we don't see her around."

"Look, she's waving at us!" I stood up. "Let's go talk to her."

"You go ahead," Nina said, not moving.

Suddenly, I remembered her ankle, and sat back down. Raising my fingers to my mouth, I let out a shrill whistle and called, "Shani!"

She dropped into the U-shaped ramp and carved some turns. Then she headed our way, grinding down a rail and popping over a curb before she screamed to a stop in front of us.

"Wow!" I exclaimed. "Where did you learn that?"

"Mostly from following my older brother around," she said, sitting down to tighten her laces. "I've only lived here for eight months. When I first moved, I only knew a few people, so my bro and I hung out a lot."

"Where are you from?" I asked.

"Depends," she said. "I was born in Africa, Kenya to be exact, but my family lived in England for six years. My dad's an engineer. The company he works for is Comet Chemicals and they transferred him to the Canadian division. He expects a transfer to Argentina in a few years."

"You sure move a lot," I said.

"That's for sure. My mom says we are citizens of the world. Sometimes it's hard, though. I barely know my cousins in Africa. But my grandmother is coming to Canada this winter. Nyanya wants to see snow. Ha! She'll be sorry."

"Take her tobogganing," I suggested.

"Nyanya, speeding down a hill." Shani laughed. "That would be a sight." She stood, and started to roll forward. "I've got to practise. I want to look decent on the big day."

I jumped to my feet. "The Skate Jam is for in-liners, too?"

She nodded. "BMXers, too."

"But that's the same day as the soccer tournament," I reminded her. "Nina is out. If you don't come …"

Shani shrugged. "I promised the other skaters I'd perform. Not many girls use the park and we want to change that. The Skate Jam is the perfect opportunity to show off some *girl power*."

"But we need you … come on, Shani."

"Sorry," she said. "I'm signed up for the freestyle competition."

Before I could argue, she skated off, calling, "See ya later!"

"This is just peachy," I snarled.

Now Nina and I were both miserable. We sulked in silence until Nina spotted Josh. She grabbed my arm. "Look, he's trying to nail that move. You know, the one where he grinds down the rail."

"Then grinds himself into the pavement," I said. We looked at each other and laughed.

Watching Josh, I suddenly became aware of the action behind him. Alison was slowly riding her bike outside the fence, staring in. A few minutes later, Shani glided over to the fence and spoke to her. Reaching into her jean shorts, Alison passed some bills through the chain link.

I nudged Nina. "That's strange. Do they know each other?

Shani is new to Glendale, they go to different schools, and they don't play on the same soccer team. What is their connection?"

Nina didn't hear me; she was concentrating on Josh's next move.

* * *

On Friday afternoon the temperature soared to over thirty degrees. Getting ready for the six o'clock game, I pulled my hair into a ponytail, removed my earrings, and dropped extra ice into my water bottle.

At the soccer field the air was still, the sun blazing. Nina sat on the team bench, ready to cheer us on to victory. Only ten girls showed up for the blue team, while our competition, the orange team, had thirteen.

Jenn was staring out at the parking lot when I walked up. "Where's Shani?" I asked. "She's never missed a game."

She tipped up her sun visor. "Practising for the Skate Jam."

I rolled my eyes. "She can practise anytime. Our soccer team plays one game a week. It's bad enough she's missing the tournament."

"A pro in-liner from Waterloo is at the skatepark tonight," Jenn said. "He's offered to share some tips. Anyway, Shani's not the problem. She's the only player who phoned me. If I knew we were going to be short girls, I'd have brought in players from another team."

"What about the tournament?" I asked. "Can we play?"

She hesitated. "I'm swamped with homework, and I've got my own soccer games. I don't know … with the lack of commitment on the team …"

"Please!" I begged. "The Kicks tournament is the best thing to happen to rec soccer ever!"

She mussed up my hair and laughed. "I'll phone the parents. If everyone is as enthusiastic as you are, I'll find the time to coach."

"Right on!" I exclaimed, punching the air. Then I went around talking up the tournament with the other players.

The orange team fielded ten players — a full squad. Their goalkeeper stood in net, loosening up. Two subs waited on the bench.

Our team had nine players on the field. No subs. Sam bravely took her place in net, preparing to get juiced. Kristi moved forward from midfield to play striker in Nina's place.

Kristi took the kickoff, booting the ball deep into the orange territory. One of their midfielders hammered it straight back at me. Hardening my muscles, I took the ball off my stomach, then fetched it and cut across the field. My right foot controlled the ball up the wing. When an orange player tried to intercept me, I kicked the ball between her legs.

Ha! I laughed to myself. Who needs two feet to dribble?

Another player ran up and began pressuring me from the side until I kicked the ball out of bounds.

"Remy!" Jenn called. I glanced over. She had two fingers raised. "You could have outrun the girl."

Easy for her to say, I thought, wiping beads of sweat from my face.

The ref signalled the orange team to take the throw-in. Standing behind the touchline, the ball raised overhead, the girl stared at one teammate, and then faked us out by throwing to another. The orange receiver trapped the ball under her foot, turned, and booted it to her midfielder.

Kristi charged after the girl as she dribbled down the middle of the field. Before she could catch up, the orange midfielder booted the ball deep into our zone. Marie ran and kicked it out of our goal area. We struggled to keep up with the orange team. Without subs, no one could take a break. Eventually, playing short-handed, with the sun beating down, we started to wilt. The soccer field felt like Death Valley.

Before the end of the half, the ref noticed our tomato coloured faces and allowed an extra water break. We gobbled up refreshing orange slices that a thoughtful parent had brought. Too tired to sit on the bench, we collapsed on the grass where Marie misted our faces with water from a spray bottle.

Nina tried to cheer us on. "Go blue. You rock!"

Five minutes later, we ran back onto the field with a burst of energy. After some nice passing, we were in position to score. Kristi took an angle shot at the net. It went wide. Running up to the ball, I aimed at the left corner. Drawing my leg back, I followed through, hard and straight, right on target. The orange goalkeeper scrambled to the left, stuck out her foot, and deflected the ball with the tip of her shoe. Kristi grabbed the rebound, but an orange defender got in her face. She fell in the struggle to hold onto the ball. The orange team blasted down the field.

Kristi stayed down. I didn't blame her; the intense action on the net had worn me out, too. But lying down on the field? Jenn would take a fit. Since the ball was tangled up at the far end, I jogged over to razz her. As I approached, she sat up and held her head in her hands. This didn't look good.

"What's wrong?" I asked, kneeling down.

"A sharp pain is shooting through my brain," she cried. "The heat — plus, I got my braces tightened today."

The ref blew the whistle, and both teams sat down on the field. Jenn came running out to attend to Kristi. After a brief discussion, Jenn walked her off the field. That left eight tired players.

I started to think, maybe Jenn is right. How can we form a team for the tournament when we can't field our regular games?

The orange team pulled ahead by a goal, then two. We didn't have enough strength to stop them. When the final whistle blew, we dragged our cooked bodies off the field. The score was 4–0.

Jenn patted us on the backs. "I'm proud of you girls. You stuck it out."

7

The Green Baggers

Five o'clock is hunting time at the O'Sullivan house. There I was, running and hopping around the yard, trying to dodge the beast's jaws. As I leaped off the deck, Tucker pounced, sinking his teeth into my running shoe.

"No!" I cried. "Stop!"

Tucker was in his wolf zone. My feet were bunnies — his supper. Never mind the fact that I had filled his bowl with crunchy kibble, and he would never have to use hunting skills. The life of a pampered pooch was not for Tucker; he was a hunter at heart.

Worried that he might ruin my shoe, I threw a stick to distract him, then jumped up on the picnic table.

"Ha ha!" I called down to him. "You can't catch me."

Barking, he dropped the stick and circled back. Determined to win the game, he ran, gaining speed, then leapt. His nimble body cleared the bench but slammed into the table slats. Yelping, he flipped backwards onto the ground.

"Poor baby!" I cried, rushing to make sure he was okay. His head popped up. He grabbed my shoe. A fake out?

Mom poked her head out the door. "Tucker needs direction. Why don't you play fetch?"

"His ball is gone," I explained. "He either buried it or ate it."

Mom held up my FIFA soccer ball. "How about this?"

Before I could stop her, she tossed the ball into the yard. Tucker roared after it, his tail wagging, his ears flapping in the wind. Since the ball was too big to fit in his mouth, he pushed it with his nose.

"Not bad!" I said, dashing after him. He galloped straight at me. As I stuck my foot out to steal the ball, he deked me out.

"Hey, where did you learn that?"

Batting the ball with his front paws, he sped off, running circles around me. The dog was teasing me, bringing the ball in close, and then rushing off when I lunged.

Before long, we were both panting for air. Tucker's tongue hung out the side of his mouth like a piece of stretch toffee. We headed inside for a drink of water where I found Mom with her head in the freezer.

"Tucker and I found a game we can play together," I told her. "It's not exactly soccer, more like a game of deke out."

"I'm glad," she said, pulling out a low-fat lasagna. "Tucker needs plenty of exercise."

While I fed Tucker his puppy kibble, Mom popped the lasagna in the microwave to thaw, then began to chop lettuce for a salad.

With a jolt I remembered Mom's mysterious meeting the night before. "Why were you at the Andrews'?" I asked.

"I went on business," she said. "It's confidential."

"But ... I'm your daughter. You can tell me, and I won't breathe a word to anyone. Promise. Are they moving?"

She reached for a tomato. "Why don't you speak to Alison?"

"You know we don't talk anymore."

"Remy," she said, firmly, "I am not free to discuss this with you."

Mom wasn't about to budge, so I tried a different angle. "I

heard Mr. and Mrs. Andrews got separated. Do you think they're going to get back together?"

"The marriage is over," Mom said, slicing a cucumber. "That much I can tell you."

Without knowing it, Mom had given me the answer. She works with a lot of couples that get divorced. Often the husband and wife have to sell the family home in order to afford two smaller places.

So that was the big secret. The Andrewses were moving. No more Alison. I should have felt happy, but it wasn't that simple. I wandered to my room and flopped on my bed.

Alison and I met in kindergarten and became instant friends. My mind drifted back to some of the crazy times we had shared, like her eighth birthday — a sleepover. All the girls fell asleep, except for the two of us. We stayed up all night daring each other to eat freezies. By morning, the package was empty and we were wired.

Last spring, we built a homemade Slip 'n Slide. Alison laid out an old tarpaulin on her sloping lawn, then set the hose across it full blast. Dressing up in garbage bags, we ran outside to slide. At that very moment, some boys from our class rode by on their bikes, hooting and hollering. Totally embarrassing! The guys called us "green baggers" for the rest of the school year.

And then there was Butterscotch, Alison's caramel-coloured bunny. She didn't act like a rabbit. In the house, she behaved cat-like, roaming freely and using a litter box. When Alison took her outside, holding Butterscotch in her arms, the neighbourhood kids went crazy.

Alison and I had been so close. How did our friendship go so wrong? To think, I had almost accused her of digging up a practice field and causing Nina's injury. Good thing I stopped myself in time. In frustration, I tossed my pillow at the wall. Maybe if I had cut her some slack when she returned from

England, things would be different now. I mean, what if Nina was right? What if Alison had a really good reason for acting horrible, and I never let her explain? Now she was going to move, and I might never see her again.

Deep down, I missed Alison. At the very least, I needed to talk to her and find out what really happened so long ago.

I still remembered her phone number. Taking a deep breath, I picked up the receiver and began to dial. Before I punched in the last digit, I chickened out. I mean, what would I say? "Hey, what's up? Thought I'd call you a year later."

Lame.

The phone rang and Mom answered it. Now that the line was tied up, I had time to think. Lying back on my bed, something else occurred to me. What if Alison didn't want to speak to me? What if she yelled or, even worse, hung up?

Perhaps phoning was not a good idea. I ran over my week's schedule in my head. Starting tomorrow: Wednesday, I had soccer practice; Thursday, piano lessons; Friday was free.

Settled. On Friday, I would go to Alison's house. No matter what happened, at least I'd know the real deal.

Smelling dinner, I leapt up and headed downstairs. Mom hung up the phone as I entered the kitchen. "That was your coach calling."

"What's up?" I asked, crossing my fingers.

"Jenn signed the team up for the Kicks' tournament. The first game starts at eight o'clock, Saturday morning, but she wants everyone on the field by seven-thirty. Each team is guaranteed two games. The two top place teams will advance to a championship match in the afternoon."

"Yes!" I punched the air.

"No snacks," Mom said, as I explored the kitchen cupboards. "Dinner will be ready in a half hour."

Dad was reading the evening newspaper when I entered the living room. Sitting down at the piano, I took out my sheet music. "A Thousand Miles," by Vanessa Carlton. My fingers danced across the keyboard with a new energy. Forgetting Dad was behind me, I sang out loud, because inside, I knew that getting together with Alison was the right move.

8

Soccer Dog

The next morning Nina was absent from school for an appointment with the physiotherapist. When she returned after lunch, she practically danced into the classroom. Now that the swelling was down, the physiotherapist was able to wrap her leg in a special tape that held her ankle like a cast. No more crutches. That made her day.

"I've got more good news," she said. "Jenn asked me to be the assistant coach until I am able to play."

"Cool," I said. "Does that mean you're coming to practice tonight?"

"Definitely," she said. "I'll pick you up."

* * *

"Steak and cake!" Dad pushed through the front door, his arms weighed down with grocery bags. "The butcher cut me three tender T-bones. The baker sliced me three pieces of Black Forest cake."

"Dad," I said, in a disapproving tone. "That's a lot of meat … and isn't cake off limits?"

"Not for a celebration!" he said, heading to the kitchen. "This afternoon your mother sold the Paisley house."

Dad couldn't fool me. He could have bought Mom flowers.

This "celebration" had a lot to do with his stomach. Still, I was impressed that Mom had sold the property. The little white house had sat on the market for months.

The owner, Mr. Paisley, had lived there for over fifty years. Recently, he moved into a nursing home and had to put his place up for sale. But there was a problem. Whenever the empty house was shown, potential buyers would not go past the strange odour in the front hall. As time passed, the stink grew. Rumours of dead bodies spread throughout the neighbourhood, the stories growing freakier by the week.

Mom shrugged off such talk. "Utter nonsense," she insisted. "I know Mr. Paisley, and he is a perfect gentleman."

But, one day, while Mom was showing the house, she happened to look up. She saw a damp, yellow spot on the ceiling. It was growing larger before her eyes. Maybe Mom didn't believe the stories, but just the same, she got freaked. No way she was going to investigate that odour.

Instead, she grabbed her cell phone and called the police. Two officers arrived, wearing masks with filters. Mom stood back while the first policeman ascended the stairs to the attic. At the top, he tipped open a wooden hatch. A hiss! A scream! The officer slammed the hatch shut and put a call in to police headquarters. "We need animal control, pronto. A raccoon family has made its home in the attic. Use caution: the mother is dangerous. She is protecting babies."

Mystery solved. The yellow stain: six months of raccoon droppings. A major gross-out! Animal control found the raccoon family a new home, far away, in a forest. The attic was cleaned, and the entire ceiling replaced. Still, the odour lingered. Who on earth would buy that home? A thought occurred to me. What if the Andrewses moved there? Alison — stuck in a stinkpot. Nasty!

At five o'clock, Mom burst through the door, singing a Beatles' tune. She even laughed when Tucker tackled her.

"Congratulations!" I called, meeting her in the hallway. "How did you sell the Paisley home?"

She winked. "The new owner has sinus problems. He can't smell a thing."

"Mom," I said, shocked. "That's not right."

"Oh, yes it is," she replied. "The man knows the history of the home, and he doesn't mind one bit. In fact, he is quite delighted, since he bought the property for a lower price. And eventually, the odour will disappear."

Her head tilted when she noticed the dining room — the fancy place settings and the bottle of red wine, sitting uncorked.

"Where's your father?" she asked, heading to the kitchen.

Before I could answer, the patio door burst open and there stood Dad, grinning. "Hi, Honey! I'm cooking a special dinner on the barbecue. When you're ready, meet me at the grill." Tucker slipped through the open doorway into the backyard.

"Dad," I called, "I have soccer practice at six."

"Lots of time," he said. "Steaks will be ready in fifteen minutes." Whistling a tune, he grabbed the barbecue sauce from the fridge and headed back outside. As he slid the patio door open, Tucker darted past him. His head was down, his teeth were clamped on something brown.

"Steak!" Dad cried. He lunged, but Tucker escaped his hands.

"Drop it," Dad ordered. "That's mine!"

No way Tucker was giving up his prize. Bounding through the living room, he galloped upstairs and out of sight.

Dad followed yelling, "Wait till I get my hands on that dog!"

We searched behind doors and in closets. When we finally discovered Tucker hiding under my double bed, all that remained of the steak was bone. He had devoured the meat in minutes. And now his jaws were set like a vise on the bone. We couldn't reach him in his low, dark, cave.

"What if he chokes?" I said, getting worried. "Steak bones are dangerous."

"Not as dangerous as a man on a diet," Dad muttered under his breath. Boy, was he ever upset. He acted as though Tucker had committed a crime.

"I'm not hungry," I lied. "And there's plenty of steak for you and Mom."

His eyes remained fixed on the bed.

"The barbecue," I reminded him.

He turned with a start. "The steaks!" He tore out of my bedroom, leaving me to deal with the dog.

I lay on the floor listening as Tucker chewed on the bone, praying he wouldn't choke. After a lot of coaxing, he finally came out, licking his chops. His tail gave a cautious wag.

I threw my arms around him. "Crazy dog! You could have burned your paws snitching food off a hot barbecue. And steak bones are bad — they can get caught in your throat."

He offered me a paw.

"I'm not mad," I said. "Whose fault was it anyway, leaving you alone with a steak at hunting time?"

At five-thirty, after I'd quickly devoured an apple, Nina knocked on my back door, wearing her soccer jersey and running shoes.

"Come in," I called through the screen. "How come you're early?"

"Jenn asked me to check the field before practice," she said. "She doesn't want more injured players."

"I'll hurry," I said, running upstairs to find my soccer socks and shoes. When I returned, Tucker's mouth was clamped down on Nina's arm.

"He's not hurting me," she observed, "but my wrist bone is making a grinding noise."

"He's excited after eating a real bone," I explained, dangling my long, blue sock in the air. Tucker dropped Nina's arm to play tug-of-war with me.

Glancing into the living room, I saw Mom and Dad sitting at the dining table, a mouth-watering steak on each plate, their wineglasses raised in a toast.

"Tucker's in trouble," I whispered to Nina. "He stole a steak from the barbecue. The only safe place for him right now is with me."

I grabbed the leash from the front hall closet, then wrote a short note, explaining that I had taken Tucker so they could enjoy a quiet dinner.

Tucker doesn't need encouragement to go outside. He spends a good part of his day staring out the window, wishing he could break through. All I had to do was open the door a crack and he bolted.

"Bye," I called, trying to hold on to the leash.

"Pick you up at seven," Dad responded. "I'll need to walk off this meal."

Along the way, Tucker strained at the leash, nearly pulling my arm out of its socket, as he surged after squirrels. Nina shuffled along like an old lady. Being in the middle, I got tugged both ways. By the time we reached the field, Tucker was wheezing for air, having half-strangled himself on the leash.

Nina's face dropped as she gazed around. "What's going on?"

"I have no idea," I said, equally confused.

More than a dozen small holes surrounded us. As we surveyed the field, a yellow Volkswagen Beetle drove into the parking lot. Jenn jumped out and grabbed the big equipment bag from her trunk.

"Hey, puppy!" she called, dropping the bag and running to Tucker. As she bent down, he stood on his hind legs, put his paws on her shoulders, and grabbed the ball cap off her head.

"You're a cutie," she cooed, yanking her cap back.

Nina poked Jenn to get her attention. "You'd better check out the field."

"What the …?" She dropped to her knees, examining a nearby hole. "Hmmm … see how one side is smooth? My guess is these holes were made with a trowel or small shovel."

"What are the holes for?" Kristi asked, running up behind. She was wearing one green and one blue sock.

Jenn sighed. "Beats me."

As more players arrived, she sent them to fill in the holes.

"We can't practise on this field," Jenn decided. "With all these freshly filled holes, the ground might be uneven. After Nina's accident, I'm not taking chances."

"The tournament is in three days," I reminded her. "We need to practise."

"Let's warm up by jogging the nature trail," Jenn suggested. "The lilies of the valley are in bloom, and the woods smell like perfume."

Tucker wagged his tail, eager to join in on the run.

As it turned out, the trail had more booby traps than the field. We picked our way over fallen branches, our cleats crunched over twigs and stones. A plank was missing from the low wooden bridge over the creek. A garter snake slithered out from a rock. I heard a bullfrog croak and was searching for it when Jenn called, "Keep moving, Remy!"

While we jogged the loop around the creek, two more players arrived and they were waiting with Nina.

"Ten girls at practice." Jenn's face beamed. "A record."

Jenn led us to the playground. At that time of the day, the

area was deserted, as most children were home eating supper. Jenn handed out beach balls and instructed us to inflate them.

"Beach party!" I cried, tossing mine in the air.

"Grab a partner," Jenn said. "We're going to practise headers."

"Why use these instead of soccer balls?" Sam asked.

"For safety," Jenn said. "In the next few minutes you're each going to head these balls about fifty times. Before I allow soccer balls, I want to make sure you are using proper technique. Otherwise, you could injure your delicate neck muscles."

"And get a major headache," Marie added.

I tied Tucker's leash to a small maple tree and joined the others.

We huddled around Jenn. "During your games, I've seen some strange headers," she said. "A few of you close your eyes and still expect to hit the ball square on the forehead."

"It's like this," I explained. "You look up and the ball's barrelling down on you. Your eyes sense danger and close automatically. It's like a blink. You can't help it."

Jenn laughed. "That's why we need to practise. Your eyes must learn that it's okay to stay open. In fact, it's safer." Next she talked about balance and timing when heading balls. Then we broke off into partners. Tucker desperately wanted to join in. Watching us play with beach balls while he was stuck to a tree drove him crazy. He bucked and barked, determined to break free and play.

After a while, we couldn't stand the noise any longer.

"Quick," Jenn said, plugging her ears, "deflate the balls before the dog goes berserk." She surveyed the area, nodding with approval. "Lots of mature trees, swings, a climber … a ready-made obstacle course."

"You should see Tucker handle the ball," I piped up. "If I take his leash off, he can demonstrate."

"Is he like the soccer dog in that movie?" Marie asked, petting him.

"Yep," I said, "except he doesn't follow the rules. He just has fun."

"Dogs aren't allowed off-leash in this park," Jenn reminded me. But I could tell by the look in her eyes that she was curious.

"No one's here but us," I said.

The rest of the team backed me up, until Jenn gave in.

"Watch this," I said, holding the ball up to Tucker. His tail began to wag, gaining speed until it was whirling in full circles.

"A jet propeller," Shani laughed, copying with her finger.

Before the dog pulled down the tree, I unsnapped the leash. He started nosing the ball, batting it around the swings with his paws.

Everyone cheered.

"Try and steal the ball from him," I dared them all. As I suspected, he deked out everyone, leaving bodies rolling on the ground.

"Wow!" Jenn exclaimed, clapping. "Such speed and tight turns. We could use him on our team."

"Yeah," I laughed, "And if this were Hollywood, it could happen."

"Better leash him now," Jenn said. "I want to show the team something new."

"Tucker!" I called.

He stopped running, raised one paw, pointed his tail, and stood like a statue, concentrating.

"Tucker," I called again. He sprang off — the wrong way.

"Come back!" I yelled, stomping my foot.

He didn't listen.

"Maybe he saw a bunny," Sam said. "They come out at dusk."

"What are you girls waiting for?" Jenn hollered. "Catch that dog!"

We tore after him. He had a strong lead, galloping like a wild stallion. He zig-zagged around a park bench, then bounded up a hill and disappeared over the other side. A startled cry pierced the air. Tucker barked excitedly. Next thing I knew, Alison and Emily came running out from the other side of the hill. Alison was holding something — some kind of metal object. It was larger than her hand, but I could tell the thing was easy to carry by the way she pumped her arms and ran full speed. I strained to get a better look, but they disappeared into the trees. I stood there stunned, not wanting to believe my eyes. But why run if they weren't guilty? My heart sank. My suspicions had come true.

9

Strange and Stranger

That was strange," Kristi said, as she watched the two girls flee. "Are they afraid of Tucker?"

"Alison and Emily both love dogs," I said, stone-faced.

"Then why are they running?" Sam asked. "Anyone can see he wants to play."

"It was them," I said, my cheeks burning. "They did it."

By them, I meant Alison. No doubt she had dragged Emily along.

"Did what?" Nina, said, shuffling up behind.

"Dug those holes to wreck our practice," I said. "If we can't practice, we can't win."

Nina gave me a look. "I don't think …"

I grabbed her arm. "Your ankle wasn't an accident."

"Get a grip," she snapped. "They wouldn't do such a thing."

"Then you explain it!"

"I can't," she admitted. "Let's ask Alison at school tomorrow."

"Oh, sure. You think she's going to confess?"

Tucker distracted me when he came prancing back. I grabbed his collar before he could bolt after new prey — a squirrel, bunny, moth, floating leaf … anything.

Snapping on the leash, I stormed over to discuss the problem with Jenn.

"Those girls behind the hill — did you see how they took off when we found them?"

"Yeah," Jenn said, picking up a ball.

"They play on the red team," I informed her. "A few weeks ago, I heard them talking about a plan to beat us in the tournament."

"It's a free world," Jenn said, nimbly juggling the ball. "They have as much right to be here as we do."

"One of them was carrying something in her hand," I pointed out.

She caught the ball and looked directly at me. "A trowel?"

I shrugged. "I couldn't tell for sure … but yes, I think so."

"Remy," she said, tossing the ball at me. "We have no proof. There's nothing we can do." Jenn called the others over. "Did anyone see what the girl was carrying?" No one could say for sure. We hadn't been close enough.

"But …"

"So far this season, we've been working on skills. Are you ready to learn some playmaking?"

Shouts of approval rang out.

"We'll start with an easy yet effective play to help us win a goal in the tournament."

Sitting in a semicircle, everyone listened closely. Listening to Jenn talk strategy made me forget about Alison.

Near the end of the practice, Tucker jumped up on his hind feet, straining against the leash, dancing around the tree. He had spotted Dad approaching. From a distance, I watched Dad untie Tucker. He got down on one knee, eye to eye with the dog. Tucker put a paw on his lap. They appeared to be having a serious talk — one-sided, of course.

After practice, I rushed over to defend my dog.

"Dad," I said, grabbing the leash. "Tucker didn't make you mad on purpose. Left alone in the backyard, he couldn't resist free food."

Dad gave me a lopsided smile. "After I cooled down," he said, "I realized something: if I were Tucker, I would have done the same thing. He smelled steak, he grabbed steak, he ate steak."

I studied his face. "You're not mad?"

"Let's just say I overreacted. Still … Tucker is more of a handful than your mother and I ever imagined."

"He is a little crazy, but we love him … right?" Dad squeezed my hand.

"Of course, he's part of our family."

That's all I needed to hear. I threw my arms around Dad and hugged him.

At home I slapped together a peanut butter sandwich and washed it down with milk. My slice of Black Forest cake sat waiting in the fridge for me. Chocolate, cherries, whipping cream — all in the same bite. Yummy! Tucker stood next to me begging and drooling. "Not a chance," I said. "You already ate my first course."

At eight o'clock there was still lots of daylight outside. Pumped about the upcoming tournament, I took my soccer ball to the backyard. Determined to improve my game, I practised dribbling with two feet. Playing against Tucker was like facing a full team. The maniac was everywhere.

I went to bed exhausted, my muscles aching from all the exercise. The house was quiet. The room was dark. But I couldn't sleep. My mind was in a swirl. How could I get proof that Alison was up to no good? There was that day at the skatepark when I caught her slipping Shani money through the fence. Shani didn't show up for the last game, and she wouldn't even consider playing in the tournament. Did Alison pay her off? Shani didn't seem like the type who could be bought. Then again, I didn't know her well. Anyway, it all added up — sort of. If I jammed a few pieces in place, I could put the puzzle together. Even if I didn't get the details exactly right, my gut told me that Alison was responsible. To think, I had almost made a fool of myself, going over to her house, trying to save our friendship.

* * *

The next day, at recess, Nina headed to the butterfly garden. Even without the crutches, she still had to baby her foot.

No way, I told myself, I'm tired of sitting around at recess, especially since Nina has been taking every side but mine lately.

Instead, I decided to shoot baskets with some classmates. As I headed to the hoops, I spotted Lucas and Josh sitting at the edge of the schoolyard, bent over the grass. They were sticking kitchen forks into the ground. Curious, I jogged over.

"If you're hungry, I'll share my lunch," I said, smirking. "You don't have to eat dirt."

Lucas put a finger to his lips "Shhh … you'll scare them away."

"Scare what away?"

"The worms," Josh said. "We're charming them." He picked up a twig and tapped the fork.

"That's pretty desperate," I said, trying to keep a straight face. "Seriously, you could do better than worms."

Josh shot me a look. "Very funny."

Lucas sat up on his knees. "If you must know, the other day I was surfing the Net looking for worm data when I stumbled upon the World Worm Charming Contest site. Each year, the event is held in a small town in England. The world record is five hundred and eleven worms in thirty minutes."

"Five hundred and eleven? You're kidding, right?"

They were serious.

"Okay, so what's with the forks? You calling them for dinner?"

"Watch," Lucas said, demonstrating. "When I hit the handle with the twig, vibrations ring through the dirt. Worms are attracted to the sound."

I dropped my head in my hands. "Lucas, you can't believe everything you read on the Net."

Josh piped up. "Worm charming is recorded in the *Guinness Book of World Records*."

I decided that basketball could wait for another day. Getting comfortable on the ground beside them, I watched them twist and twang on their forks.

When the bell finally rang, I said, "Told you so. Big surprise. No worms."

They ignored me. They were both stuck in their own strange world, talking back and forth.

"I read that the competitors used 'garden forks,'" Josh said. "Whatever that is."

"Could be a pitchfork," I said, breaking into their conversation, "or a smaller weeding fork."

Lucas's eyes widened. "She's right! Small details make all the difference." He turned back to Josh. "Meet me at my place after school. We'll grab a pitchfork from the garden shed and try again."

"Let's experiment with twigs, too," Josh said. "I bet different shapes and sizes create unique vibrations."

Lucas acting weird I could understand. But Josh?

On the way into the school, I caught up with Nina. "Get this," I said. "Josh and Lucas were charming worms during recess."

"Cool," she said. "You should have come and got me."

"Nina, did you hear me?"

She shrugged. "In India, there are men who charm king

cobra snakes. And those snakes are deadly poisonous. Makes sense to start with worms."

Oh, brother. Was I the only normal person?

* * *

After school, Tucker came to greet me at the front door. My soccer ball hung from his mouth.

How cute, I thought. He wants to play. Wait a sec. The ball shouldn't fit in his mouth. Staring, I noticed the ball looked deflated.

"You … you bit through my best ball! Bad dog!"

Dad came around the corner, his hand motioning me to quiet down. "We have company, Remy," he said, sounding strangely formal.

Growling at Tucker, I followed Dad to the living room. The dog followed, prancing with the ball in his mouth. I didn't bother to take it away — it was ruined anyway.

"Hi, Remy," Mom said, with an exaggerated smile. "This is Mrs. Whitfield, the psychologist we told you about."

Huh? No one told me about a psycho-whatever! A lady, whom I had never seen before, removed her glasses, and smiled at me.

True, I don't always act like a perfect angel, and my grades had slipped this year … but this came out of the blue.

"Hi, Remy." She stood to shake my hand. I shoved my own hand into my pocket. "I would like to speak with you for a few minutes, if you don't mind."

Yes, I did mind. Stepping back defensively, I narrowed my eyes. "About what?"

"Please, sit, Remy," Mom said, firmly. "This is important. Mrs. Whitfield needs your cooperation."

I perched forward on the piano bench, preparing to bolt if

things got any stranger. Tucker sat at my feet, happily chewing on the ball.

Mrs. Whitfield took out a notebook and pen. "Let's start with the important issues. How does Tucker greet you? Your mom tells me he's a bit rough."

"Tucker? What does he have to do with this?"

Mom shot Dad a look. "Didn't you tell her?"

He shook his head. "Didn't you?"

"Tell me what?" I said, shifting uncomfortably.

"Mrs. Whitfield is a *dog* psychologist," Mom explained, a grin spreading across her face. "Oh, dear … you thought …"

Next thing I knew, the whole room started chuckling — everyone that is, but me. I blushed crimson. Not funny!

As it turned out, my parents had called an animal psychologist, believing Tucker had a hyperactive disorder. Over the next hour, Mrs. Whitfield spent time alone with Tucker, and she also observed how Tucker behaved with each family member. Mrs. Whitfield asked me to knock on the front door, so she could see how Tucker greeted me. As usual, he took a running leap and pounced.

"Just as I expected," she said, nodding. "He is showing his love. That is how wild dogs greet members of their pack. Of course, that behaviour is not acceptable in the human world. With some work, you can teach him a new way to say hello."

When the hour was up, Mrs. Whitfield gave her shocking diagnosis: "Tucker's behaviour is normal."

My parents' jaws dropped.

Mrs. Whitfield explained, "All puppies are filled with energy. And certain breeds, such as Springer Spaniels, come into this world supercharged, ready to go, go, go! If you've ever watched two puppies at play, you will observe plenty of biting and tackling, snapping and growling. I suggest a puppy friend for

Tucker. Also, I will give you directions to a wonderful park at the edge of town called Rover's Realm, a place where dogs can run off-leash. Of course, obedience school is absolutely necessary as your dog is strong-willed. I assure you, with proper training, Tucker will become a well-behaved member of the family."

Mom still wasn't convinced. She told Mrs. Whitfield how Tucker ripped apart the metal bars on his cage, and that he howls every time we leave him.

"A mild case of separation anxiety," Mrs. Whitfield said. "I can offer ways to help Tucker at our next appointment."

Translation: Tucker loves his family so much that he can't bear to be without us. How cute is that!

10

Kickoff

A purple hand reached across my desk.

"Ew … get away!"

"I need to borrow this," Lucas said, grabbing my black marker.

"Next time, ask first," I said, turning around. "What's up with your hands? Did your latest experiment go wrong?"

"Mulberries," he said. "My neighbour's tree is bursting with them. He's happy when I pick them since fallen berries make a real mess on the sidewalk."

"Mulberries go in your mouth, not on your hands," I pointed out.

"Want some?" He brought a zip-lock bag out of his desk.

My stomach growled at the sight of fresh berries. Reaching in the bag, I popped one in my mouth. "Mmmm … good."

"Mulberries contain protein," Lucas explained, "plus vitamins and minerals. But if you eat too many, they become a laxative."

Laxative — a dirty word! My face twisted in disgust. From the look of his hands, I figured he had eaten a bunch.

Oh, yuck! I thought. Lucas must be all loosey-goosey on the inside. And by the deep stain on his hands, he doesn't appear to be a hand-washer.

Mental note: never touch the black marker again.

"Why do you have to analyze everything?" I said, rolling my eyes. "Can't you just enjoy the flavour?"

"You wouldn't understand," he said, zipping up the bag.

"You're right. Hey, speaking of weird — charmed any worms lately?"

"Still working on the technique," he said. "Yesterday, I whittled an apple branch. Once I fine-tune that stick, I'm sure it will make good vibrations with the fork. The worms won't be able to resist the sweet music."

"Oh, pleeeeease!" I said, turning away.

To entertain myself, I stared at the clock, watching the little hand lurch forward with each passing minute. The countdown was on. In one hour and forty-seven minutes, school would be over. Goodbye Grade 7!

Unbelievably, Mr. Jackson was still making us work, although he called it "fun."

How fun is colouring a map of the world? And what is the point when it's not going to be marked?

At two o'clock Mr. Jackson instructed us to clear out our desks. Finally! Most classes had emptied their desks the day before and were celebrating. Even with the door shut, I could hear the parties down the hall. With any luck, Mr. Jackson would let the grade sevens chill for the last hour.

We stuffed our backpacks to the breaking point, then sat at our desks and waited. Finally Mr. Jackson said the magic words: "Time for fun."

Cheers filled the air.

"Quiet," he said, pressing the air down with his hands. "I have prepared a pop quiz, consisting of information you studied over the year. Let's divide the class into two teams."

Loud groans replaced the cheers. "Can't you cut us some slack?" Josh asked, slumping over.

Mr. Jackson looked hurt. "I worked on the quiz for three nights. What could be more fun than a challenge?"

The last hour of the last day and our class was expected to use our brains. Some celebration. Oh, well, the quiz gave me time to think. While others were popping out answers, my mind wandered. Our regular Friday night game was cancelled, but tomorrow morning the Kicks soccer tournament would get underway. Since I couldn't get proof that Alison had been sabotaging our team, I made the mature decision to put her out of my mind. Anyway, she wouldn't dare try anything else — not after she almost got caught.

Pretty pathetic, I thought. Alison will do anything to win and she doesn't care if she hurts others. I smiled to myself, feeling good about my decision.

* * *

Early the next morning, my team assembled on field number seven to warm up. Thirteen players had showed up. For once, we had two subs. Our opposition, the yellow team, jogged around the far end. They also had thirteen players. Anything was possible. I mean we really could win this tournament.

A north wind blew brisk and cool. High, wispy clouds streaked across a pale blue sky. My parents sat at their usual spot, drinking coffee under a large sun umbrella. Yes, it was going to be a great day.

Marie came running from the parking lot with her father in tow. "Fresh Benny's Bagels!" she called.

The team responded enthusiastically, but before we could dig in, Jenn grabbed the bag. Thanking Marie's father, she placed them aside. "Enjoy these after the game," she insisted. "I don't want to deal with any stomach cramps."

"Doubt we'll even work up a sweat," Kristi commented. "The yellow team is in sixth place."

"Good," I said. "An easy game. We can save our energy for the red team."

Before the game, Jenn approached me. "Would you like to take the coin toss?"

"Yes," I jumped up and headed over to the ref. Usually, Nina got that privilege. My "heads" call won the toss, and I chose to begin the game playing against the north wind. That way our team would gain the "wind" advantage in the second half.

The ref blew the whistle, signalling us to take our positions. We wandered onto the field, laughing and goofing off. The field had been freshly mowed, the dry grass felt crunchy underfoot.

The yellow team took the kickoff. Assuming they'd be easy to defeat, we started off playing lazy. After all, it *was* early in the morning, and the opposition *was* down in the standings.

A pass came straight to Kristi. She stuck out her foot and hit air.

"Eye on the ball!" Jenn called.

Deep in our zone, Marie cleared the ball to the middle, setting up a goal shot for the yellow team. Fortunately, their striker botched the kick.

"Clear the ball to the wing!" Jenn called, pacing back and forth.

A few plays later, a yellow midfielder got control of the ball and dribbled it halfway down the field, unguarded.

"Cover her!" Jenn yelled. At this rate, our coach would soon be going hoarse.

The yellow player booted the ball high. It soared directly overhead. "Mine!" I called, getting in position to head it. Remembering Jenn's advice, I kept my eyes open. Problem is, I didn't like what I saw. The missile was jetting high and hard. What was I thinking?

I was no World Cup player. At the last second, I ducked out of the way. Before I could reach the bouncing ball, a yellow player appeared, her feet outsmarting mine to the ball.

If we keep playing like this, we're going to lose, I told myself. We could go down in the first round. *Not* okay!

Determined to win the ball back, I grabbed the girl's jersey and stuck my foot out to steal the ball. She fell.

The ref blew her whistle.

Only a few minutes into the game, and I had already fouled another player. The ref called a major penalty, awarding the yellow team a direct free kick on our net — a golden opportunity for them to score.

Five of our players stood side by side forming a wall in front of the net.

"Stand closer," Sam called. "I need all the help I can get." She shifted her weight back and forth in goal, fanning her arms. Still, she looked small compared to the massive net.

The yellow kicker trained her eyes on the ball. Standing back at an angle, she ran up and booted the ball, causing it to spin high and hard. Sam jumped, thrusting her gloved hand out. The rocketing ball blasted through her fingertips and into the net.

Applause rang out for the yellow team.

Sam sank onto the ground.

"Don't feel bad," Marie said, running over. "That was an impossible shot."

The team didn't speak as we walked to centre field.

"Subs!" Jenn called from the bench.

I slunk off the field.

At halftime, Jenn sat down with us on the grass.

"You girls learned a lesson," Jenn said. "Always take the competition seriously. But look, we're only down by one goal. If you work hard, we can still win."

"What about the secret play," Kristi asked, "the one you taught us at practice?"

"Watch for my hand signal," Jenn said, winking. "When I raise three fingers, make your move."

We started the second half with a new attitude. The strong north wind helped launch our kickoff deep into the yellows' territory. One of their midfielders kicked the ball back our way. For a while, the ball got volleyed back and forth between teams, neither side gaining ground. That changed when a teammate made a perfect pass to Kristi.

Jen raised three fingers. "Go for it!" she called.

Kristi and I made eye contact. She dribbled the ball to the corner of their net. Two yellow defenders raced at her, preparing to block her shot on goal. But instead, she kicked the ball across the front of the net to my waiting foot. I snapped an angle kick at the goal. The yellow goalkeeper darted across the net — but not fast enough. Goal! "Awesome fake-out!" Kristi called.

The crowd cheered for the blue team this time.

Later in the game, we tried the same play and scored. Once the yellow team's coach caught on, they squashed our move. Too late. We won 2–1.

After the handshakes, our team walked over to the tournament chart posted on the side of the washrooms hut. Our next game was scheduled for ten o'clock on field eight, against the purple team. Or … wait. Mrs. Jenkins, the convenor, licked her finger, rubbed out number eight, and wrote in *three*. Good thing we stuck around to see the change in fields. My eyes slipped down the chart, searching for the red team. As I expected, they had won their first game.

The team had a half hour to relax and eat bagels before gathering for the next game. Choosing a chocolate-chip one, I went and sat with my parents. Neither mentioned the penalty. Good. I wasn't in the mood for a lecture. I felt bad enough about my dumb move without having them rub it in.

"Whoever wins next game plays in the final," I told them. "The purple team is good, but we've beat them before."

Dad thumped me on the back. "We'll be cheering."

Before long, I noticed my team gathering on field three. "Got to go," I said, standing. "Remember, you're taking me and Nina to the Skate Jam. She's coming to the field after her physiotherapist appointment."

Mom nodded. "Good luck," she called, as I jogged off. "Watch those fouls!"

Ugh! She *had* to say it.

Jenn gathered us together for a pep talk. "In the last game, you played like you were asleep," she said. "My watch says nine forty-five. Is everyone awake?"

"Yes!" we cheered.

"I feel stronger after eating a bagel," I commented.

"Me too," Sam said. "Let's hear it for *bagel power*!"

"Whatever works!" Jenn said, laughing. "Now, remember to play your positions and play clean. With every win, the competition gets tougher. We can't afford any penalties."

Thankfully, she didn't single me out.

Jenn held a hand up. "High-fives, all around." We stood and slapped each other's hands. "No matter what happens on the field, all I ask is that you give it your best shot and have fun."

I walked out onto the field with Kristi. "I'm pumped to win," I said, punching the air.

"Me too!" she cried.

Everyone must have felt the same because the whole team played amazingly well. I even dribbled with two feet some of the time. That impressed Jenn — and me. Nina showed up partway through the second half to cheer us on. We beat the purple team: 3–1.

After the game, Mom offered me carrot sticks and celery. "Mom," I explained. "The team is meeting at Kicks."

"Fine," she said. "Eat your vegetables first." Kindly, I shared them with Dad, who didn't want them any more than I did.

"Ciao!" Luigi greeted me, as I ran into the ice cream hut.

My teammates had pulled two tables together and were sitting around talking when I arrived.

"When's the next game?" I asked pulling up a chair.

"Two o'clock," Marie said. "We get a long lunch break."

"What team are we playing?"

Crossing my fingers, I chanted to myself: not red, not red, not red.

"Don't know yet," Sam called, from across the table. "The red and black teams are still playing."

I grabbed Nina. "Let's go watch. And after, my parents will drive us to the Skate Jam. I don't have to be back at the field until one-thirty."

"I can't," she said, pulling back. "My parents are taking me to Bombay Gardens for lunch.

"But we're supposed to go to the Skate Jam together, remember?"

"How could I forget?" Nina said. "Josh reminds me every day. Bombay Gardens has a takeout window. I'll eat quickly and meet you at the skatepark entrance. My family wants to watch Josh too."

Nina left to find her parents, and I hurried to check out the game.

A couple of girls from my team joined me at the sidelines. With two minutes left in the game, the score was 7–1. A slaughter. We would face the red team in the final game for sure now.

My parents walked up as the whistle blew. "Let's go," Dad said. "Thought you were in a hurry."

"Be right there," I said, unzipping my soccer bag. "I want to change out of my cleats."

As we walked off the field, I noticed Alison and Emily a few steps ahead. Hearing excitement in their voices, I increased my stride until I got within earshot.

"Did you hear the blue team won?" Emily said. "My friend on the purple team played them last game. She says they're tough — even without Shani and Nina."

Alison nudged her. "My dad is bringing our secret weapon."

"Awesome!" Emily shrieked, jumping. "We'll win for sure!"

Shocked, I fell back in step with my parents. A secret weapon! What could it be? If Alison could dig up our field, there was no telling how low she might sink. And to think her father was in on her foul plan. My blood boiled. One thing was certain: my ears didn't lie. Alison would not get away with this — and I would make sure. But how?

"Uh … I have to go to the washroom," I told my parents, ducking off. I needed time to think.

What to do … what to do … what to do …?

On the way, I stopped by the tournament chart. The red team had been entered in the finals category, right over the blue team. We were scheduled to play on field number one. The black marker lay on the table beneath the chart. Suddenly, I got an idea. My eyes scanned the surrounding area. Mom and Dad were walking toward the parking lot. The red team was huddled with their coach over by the concession booth. I was alone. But at any moment, the red team would head over to the chart to check the time and field number for the final game.

Did I dare? Mrs. Jenkins made it look easy.

I licked the tip of my finger and placed it over the first 0 in 2:00. A quick stroke and it disappeared. It was easy! I picked up the erasable marker and inserted a three in its place. Just like that, I had changed the game time from two o'clock to two-thirty. Dropping the marker like a hot tamale, I hightailed it to the car.

11

First Annual Skate Jam

Nina and her family were already waiting at the skatepark entrance when we arrived. A green banner with the words "First Annual Skate Jam" was draped over the gate. Cartoon caricatures of skaters in various poses were duct-taped along the fence.

"What took you so long?" Nina asked when I ran up. "We could have enjoyed a sit-down meal rather than gulping our food in the car."

"You're not going to believe this," I began. "As I was leaving the field, I overheard Alison and Emily …"

I paused, contemplating. What if Nina didn't understand? She hadn't so far …

"Go on," she said, tapping her good foot.

Even though my plan was about justice — getting even — it was hard to explain, especially to Nina.

"Uh-h-h … they were bragging, as usual."

She tilted her head. "What does that have to do with you being late?"

"Look!" I exclaimed, changing the subject. "Razor is butting in line at the bowl."

Nina made a face. "Check out the symbols on his shirt."

"Skulls and snakes," I observed. "Creepy."

"Let's head over to the rails," Nina suggested. "Bet we'll find Josh there."

First, we found our families good seats in the bleachers. Sita was begging to hang out with her sister. Thank goodness Mrs. Patel insisted that she stay in the bleachers. Nina and I wanted to cruise the park on our own.

Sure enough, we found Josh standing in line at the rail. He was wearing a brown headband marked with Chinese symbols.

"What does it mean?" Nina asked.

"Courage," he replied, stone-faced.

Nina and I stood back to watch.

"Hope Josh doesn't slam," I said, crossing my fingers. "He's worked so hard."

The guy ahead of Josh attempted to ride the rail on in-line skates. He bailed partway down, landing hard on his side. Josh was up next. He ollied up onto the rail. Then came the hard part. Crouching, he began to grind down the thin bar. His face went rigid, deep in concentration, as he attempted the difficult balancing act.

"Go, Josh," I said, under my breath. "You can do it."

In a split second, his board hit the ground. He was still in control. Josh had nailed the rail! Picking up his board, he kissed the deck. Nina and I screamed like crazy.

He waved us over. "The vert competition is about to start," he said. "Skeeter's routine takes less than a minute. Hurry, we don't want to miss him."

Good thing Nina was able to run now, although the physiotherapist insisted her ankle needed more time to heal before she could play soccer. Following Josh, we snaked our way around the obstacle course of ramps, rails, and curbs. A large crowd had gathered to watch the vertical competition. Seeing skaters loop and twist high in the air is totally rad, and the vertical is by far the most popular event. We climbed to the top of the bleachers to get a good view.

"Way to go, Stephen!" a man next to us hollered.

"That's Skeeter's father," Josh said.

"His real name is Stephen?" I said. "Who would have figured? That name is so normal." I trained my eyes on the half-pipe. "Where is he?"

Josh pointed to the ground where Skeeter was talking to another skater. "Looks like we missed the best performance of the day."

"Well, let's hope the people from the X-Juice Company caught his routine," I said.

Below us, a teenager holding a megaphone announced: "The kick-flip contest will begin in ten minutes. Get down and show us your gnarly moves."

A girl from a local skate shop was handing out prizes: T-shirts, ball caps, skate magazines, stuff like that. In another area of the park, a man was flinging stickers into a crowd. The kids were going wild, lunging through the air after them.

"Battling each other for a sticker?" Nina said. "What gives?"

"Skaters stick them on helmets, boards, backpacks, whatever. The skate graphics are way cool."

Suddenly, I saw it. "The X-Juice booth!" I cried and tugged on Josh's and Nina's arms. "Let's go!"

"Don't bother." Josh made a sour face. "X-Juice is one bad brew."

"Come on," I said. "No company would make a nasty tasting drink."

"Bet?" he said, challenging me. "And besides, check out the guy behind the table. He's wearing a superhero mask. That's so lame."

"What do you mean?" I said. "Look around. I see a skater

wearing red shorts with suspenders and no shirt. Over by the bowl someone is wearing a tie over a T-shirt."

"So?" Josh said, not getting my point.

"The company wants the vendor to look different," I explained. "Anyway, who cares? The sign says the proceeds go to the skatepark. A loonie for every drink purchased will help buy a new rail. Just think Josh, no more lineups."

"Doesn't matter," he said shoving a finger down his throat. "Can't stomach the stuff."

"What flavour is it?" Nina asked.

He shrugged. "Reminded me of my mom's cranberry-covered meatloaf."

"Well, I'm going to decide for myself," I said.

"Feel free," Josh said, grabbing his skateboard. "I'm heading to the kick-flip contest. Don't want to miss out on the prizes." He stood, then sat back down again. "Before I go, how did your team do in the tournament?"

"Good," I said. "We won both games."

"Our team is in the finals," Nina said. "How cool is that?"

Suddenly, it hit me. There would be no final game. The red team would get defaulted when they didn't show for the game. The blue team would be awarded first prize and there would be no real winner. What had I done?

"You don't look happy," Josh noted.

Payback should have felt good. Why did my stomach feel sick?

I reminded myself that Alison deserved to get disqualified. But what about the rest of the red team? They hadn't done anything wrong. And what about my team? First prize wouldn't be nearly as sweet if we won by default. If only I hadn't picked up that marker.

12

The Truth Bites

Caught up in the excitement at the skatepark, I was able to push my dark thoughts to the back of my mind. Nina and I climbed down from the bleachers and headed to the X-Juice booth.

"Just 'cause Josh doesn't like X-Juice, that doesn't mean anything," I told her. "He's a picky eater — doesn't even like pepperoni on pizza."

"Look," she giggled, as we approached. "The vendor is just a kid, and he's wearing a Batman mask."

Stepping up to the table, I examined the disposable cups that had been set out. They were filled with a grayish pink liquid. The drink was thick like a milkshake.

Nina stuffed her money back in her shorts. "On second thought, I'm not thirsty. I'll try a sip of yours."

I almost changed my mind, too. Then I noticed a stack of questionnaires. I read the one on top:

Fill in your age and gender. Then answer the following questions:

1. Did you enjoy the flavour?
2. Would you purchase this drink again?
3. What is your favourite colour?

I turned Nina. "What does my favourite colour have to do with anything?"

She shrugged. "Maybe the company wants to produce X-Juice in the most popular colour. After all, the current colour needs major help."

"Good thinking." Questionnaire in hand, I placed a loonie on the table and picked up a cup. The vendor nodded mutely, his hands stuffed in his pockets.

"Thanks," I said, walking off.

Not much of a salesman, I thought.

Cautiously, I lifted the cup to my nose. "Smells fresh, but strange."

"Go ahead," Nina coaxed. "How bad can it be?"

She was right, of course. Tipping the cup back, I took a swig. Hmmm … the beverage tasted sweet and bitter at the same time. Fruity … and some other flavour I couldn't identify.

Realizing I had survived the first sip, Nina grabbed the cup. "Let me try." Swirling the mixture around in her mouth, she looked thoughtful. All of a sudden, she clicked her fingers and blurted, "Chicken!"

I laughed. "Who's ever heard of chicken in a sport drink? Glancing at the questionnaire, I suddenly realized I couldn't fill it out. "I don't have a pencil."

Back at the X-Juice booth, the vendor was posing for two little kids who thought he was a real superhero.

"Do you have a pencil?" I asked, once he was free.

He shook his head.

"How am I supposed to answer the questions?"

He shrugged, wedging his hands in his pockets.

Nina stepped forward. "My friend and I are trying to guess the ingredients. Could you please help us?"

He garbled something I couldn't understand.

"Excuse me," she said. "Could you speak up? We can't hear you."

Nina and I grinned at each other. Batman was definitely from a different world.

"The ingredients?" Nina persisted.

Beads of sweat began to form around the edge of his mask. Removing a hand from his pocket, he mopped his face.

My mouth dropped. "Your hand!" I cried. "It's purple!" Storming around the table, I grabbed the mask, exposing the one and only Lucas Baxter. "Y-you made X-Juice! And I drank it." My stomach lurched. "What did you put in that drink?!"

"Don't get so hot," he said, finding his voice.

"Five seconds," I threatened. "Either tell us, or I'm fetching the policeman at the gate."

"Mulberries," he blurted.

Nina cornered him on the other side of the table. "What else?"

"Dandelion tea. I washed and boiled the leaves myself."

"Is that all?" I asked, the threat remaining in my voice.

"A bit of honey and salt. X-Juice is sterilized for your protection. Now back off. You wouldn't understand."

"Try me," I challenged.

"This is my science project," he said, with a dramatic sweep of his arms. "Months of research and physical labour went into creating an inexpensive nutritional drink. But in order for my project to be successful, I needed human trials — to find out if the public appreciated the taste. The Skate Jam was coming up, so I …"

"Stop," I said, slicing through the air with my hand. "You tricked people into testing your nasty invention."

"But I did it in the name of science."

"Give me a break," I growled. "You did it in the name of Lucas. You were desperate to win that trip to science camp."

He shrugged. "That too. But I'm not making money. The

profits go to the skatepark. I'm helping the skaters and myself."

"Ever heard of *false advertising*?" Nina said, stepping up. "Our friend, Skeeter, was hoping the executives from X-Juice would sponsor him once they saw his routine."

"Oh … I hadn't thought of that," he said, sheepishly.

Lucas had gone too far this time. What would the skaters do when they found out — especially a guy like Razor? Yikes! Even Lucas didn't deserve that fate. "Look, Lucas," I said. "If you pack up your project and disappear, we won't tell anyone. I'm afraid that if the skaters find out it won't be pretty."

Lucas held up his money box. "They'll be happy when I present them with the cash."

Nina shook her head. "No one likes to be deceived."

His face sank. I think he finally understood.

While Lucas was packing up his booth, I nudged Nina. "Actually, the whole X-Juice thing is funny in a warped way. Leave it to Lucas. What a strange brew." I took a sip of X-Juice and sloshed it around in my mouth.

"Tastes odd," I said, "but in a healthy way."

Nina quietly looked on. All of a sudden, her eyes narrowed. Snatching the cup from my hands, she took a sip, then spat. "Something's fishy. The ingredients don't add up."

She stormed over to Lucas, pointing a finger. "What else is in that drink?"

I wiped the thick pink moustache off my lips and paid attention. Nina wouldn't go off on someone without good reason.

He didn't answer, just kept stacking the cups into a box.

"I taste chicken," Nina insisted.

"Must be the organic protein," he mumbled.

Protein? My mind wandered back to the classroom, to another time when Lucas was telling me about …

"Worms!" I screeched.

Lucas ducked behind the table. "They're freshly dug from the park and well cooked," he blurted.

"No-o-o!" Spitting out all traces, I rubbed my lips until they hurt.

Nina looked like she might throw up.

"You asked for it!" I said, shaking my fist. "I'm telling everyone what you did! And Razor is first on my list."

Lucas rushed to pack his wagon.

"Let's get out of here," Nina said, pulling me away. "This place stinks. Besides, I want to watch Shani."

We found her talking to a guy on a BMX bike. Nina and I leaned against the fence, waiting 'till she was free. For some reason, we looked at each other and cracked up.

"Can you believe Lucas?" Nina squealed. "Like, how did he get all those worms?"

"Maybe Prince Charming charmed them out of the ground," I quipped.

"Or maybe he visited the local bait man," she said, pushing me playfully. "I hear that guy electrifies the ground to get the worms to the surface."

"Zapped worms," I said. "Yummy." Laughter bubbled up again, and I doubled over, hanging onto the fence.

"Wait," Nina said, trying to catch her breath. "I remember … Lucas said he dug them up in the park."

I inhaled sharply, my laughter strangling in my throat. "What park?"

"He didn't say." She paused. "Why? What's wrong?"

"Nothing," I lied. "I just thought of something. Be right back."

"Wait, where are you going?" As I ran off, I heard her call, "I'll be sitting with Sita."

I caught up to Lucas near the entrance. His eyes were downcast as he trudged out of the skatepark, towing his wagon.

"Wait!" I called, panting. "Where did you dig up the worms?"

"At the park," he said, not bothering to stop. "Don't freak. You won't get sick. City council banned pesticides at Cedar Glen."

"Cedar Glen?" I nearly choked.

He nodded. "What's the big deal?"

"What did you use to dig up the worms?"

"A trowel."

"No!" I cried. "Tell me you didn't!"

He stopped and stared at me. "Remy, are you feeling okay? You look terrible."

"This is important," I said, meeting his stare. "Did you find the worms in the field by the forest?"

"Nope," he replied. "By the creek."

A cry of happiness burst from my lungs. "Yes! Yes! Yes!"

I was about to hug Lucas when he added, "I dug some sample holes on the field and came up dry."

"Oh, Lucas," I whimpered. "Did you fill in the holes?"

He put a hand to his mouth thinking. "Umm … I think so. Actually, maybe I forgot a few."

The truth hit me like one of Tucker's body slams. Wham! Alison and Emily did not dig the holes.

Shani! I needed to talk to her. I found her in line at a ramp.

"We've go to talk," I said, whirling her around in her skates. "It's important!"

"I'll miss my turn," she said, annoyed.

"This won't take long," I promised. "Last week when Nina and I came to watch the practice, Alison handed you money through the fence. What was that for?"

"Not that it's any of your business," she said, "but she owed me for her paper route. I took it over the week she played in the music festival."

"You know Alison?"

"Sure," she said. "We went to soccer camp in England together. Crazy, eh!"

Another slam! How could I have been so wrong? Alison hadn't done any of the rotten things of which I had accused her. As for her "secret weapon," it could be anything. Come to think of it, our team had a secret weapon — the goal-winning play that Jenn had taught us at practice.

A shudder ran through me. Gulping for air, I hid my face in my hands and cried. Wait, I told myself, choking back the tears. It's not too late. Maybe I can make things right.

Rushing to the phone booth inside the park, I dialled Alison's number. Three rings. When she answered, I would explain that there had been an error in game time and … five rings. "Come on, Alison, I breathed into the receiver. "Pick up."

The answering machine switched on.

Grabbing the phone book, I quickly looked up Emily's number. On the second ring her older brother answered.

"May I speak to Emily?" I blurted.

"Hold on." Precious seconds passed while I waited on the line. Finally, someone picked up. Her brother again. "She's out for lunch."

"Do you know where?" I probed.

"Nope," he said. "You wanna leave a message?"

"There's no time," I said, letting the receiver drop back into place.

Now what? I asked myself. I don't know anyone else on the red team. Squeezing my arms around my chest, I felt my throat tighten. Loud sobs rocked my body as I slumped to the floor.

13

Lost and Found

I heard a knock on the phone booth. Glass framed me in on all sides, leaving me no place to hide. Pressing my hand against my mouth, I tried to muffle my sobs.

"Remy, what's wrong?" Nina called.

"Everything!" I bawled.

Her eyes widened. "Whatever happened, we can fix it."

"No! *We* can't!"

"Come on, Remy," she said, "you're scaring me." She hesitated. "Should I get your parents?"

"Not that!" I buried my face in my hands.

She leaned against the glass. "Then let's find someplace private and talk."

"Go away! Once you find out what I did, you won't want to stick around."

A lady walked up to use the phone, forcing me out. Training my eyes on the ground, I burst into the skatepark.

Nina pulled me behind the bleachers. "We're alone," she said. "What's got you crazy? Tell me."

I pulled away. "No, you'll hate me."

Nina folded her arms. "We're friends, right?"

I half nodded.

"We've had a ton of good times. So when bad stuff happens,

we don't bail, we deal."

I swallowed back the lump in my throat. "You won't like what I'm going to say," I warned, wiping my eyes.

She didn't budge.

"I did something terrible."

"Go on," she coaxed.

"I overheard Alison and Emily talking about a secret weapon that they were going to use in the final game."

"What did you do?" Nina asked calmly.

"Y-you know the tournament chart?"

She nodded, keeping her eyes fixed on me.

"I … I changed the game time. Now the red team is going to show up late and get disqualified." Instead of shock or anger, it was sadness I saw on Nina's face. I looked away, unable to bear the look in her eyes.

"But why?" she asked.

"To get back at Alison. I honestly believed that she dug those holes. And I blamed her for your sprained ankle and for Shani not coming to the tournament." I let out a heavy sigh. "But I know now that I was wrong. And even if I had been right … what was I thinking messing with an official schedule? I … I tried to phone Alison and Emily to make things right, but they aren't home."

Nina thought for a moment. "You have no choice," she said, finally. "You have to tell Jenn."

"I can't," I whimpered. "I'm afraid." I looked up at my perfect friend and sighed. "You wouldn't understand. You'd never do such a thing."

There was a long silence, then Nina said quietly, "Yes I would … and I did."

I stared disbelieving. "Give me a break. Like, I believe you."

"It's true," she said. "Last year, Emily sat in front of me in

Mrs. Johnson's class. The night before a science test, I went to dance school. Besides ballet, I was enrolled in international dance, remember? That night, the instructor taught us an ancient Indian dance.

"It was so amazing, so fun, I got caught up in the dance, I forgot to study." Nina looked away. "My parents have never seen me get a grade below 'A.' I didn't want to disappoint them. So when the test was handed out, I copied off Emily's paper."

I let out a long breath. "Nina, your crime is not in the same league as mine. Lots of kids have made that mistake."

"Wait, there's more," she insisted. "The next day Mrs. Johnson accused Emily of cheating. After all, Nina Patel, perfect student, would never do such a thing, right?" Nina bit her lip. "I never came clean. In fact, until now, I've never told anyone."

I didn't know what to say. My perfect friend was not so *perfect*. But that didn't matter to me. She was brave enough to tell me her darkest secret, so I wouldn't feel like the only candidate for Creep of the Year award. At that moment, I felt closer to Nina than ever.

"My parents are shopping for a new couch this afternoon," Nina said. "We'll go back to the soccer park together, and no matter how bad things get, I'll stick with you."

"Promise?"

"Superglue."

I hugged her hard. Nina Patel — best friend ever.

During the car ride, I pressed my face against the window and rode in silence. Mom tried to make conversation, choosing the worst possible topic: the tournament. Nina did her best to take the heat off by chatting about the new perfumery at the mall. Still, Mom suspected something. She trained her eyes on me in the rear-view. A worry line creased her forehead.

When we pulled up to the soccer park, I sensed that Mom

was about to corner me, forcing out my dark confession. Grabbing my soccer bag, I ran off, calling, "See ya."

Although I knew my parents were planning to stay and watch the game, I couldn't deal with them, too. Straight ahead on field number one, I spotted my team gathering by the bench. My knees went weak. "What do you think will happen?" I asked Nina.

She gave me a reassuring smile. "The ref will probably delay the game until the other team arrives."

"Do you think Jenn will let me play?"

"Maybe not." She patted me on the back. "But you can sit with me, and we'll cheer the team on together."

Nina had a way of making the next few minutes seem possible.

Jenn was consulting her clipboard when we walked up.

"Go," Nina said, pushing me ahead. Reaching behind, I grabbed her hand. "Glue," I said. "Remember?"

We approached Jenn, side by side. She looked up and smiled. "Nina, I'm glad you're here. I could use help on the bench for the big game."

"Uh … yeah," she said, looking flustered.

"Strange," Jenn said, looking around. "No one from the red team is here yet. I figured they'd arrive early, especially for the championship game."

Nina nudged me. "Tell her."

At the same time, a little voice inside me screamed, "Run! Save yourself!"

I pulled Nina away. "I can't do it. I've changed my mind. No one has to know what I did." I cast about for an excuse. "No one knew what you did, right?"

"But you will," she said. "Trust me, the feeling stinks. Every time I see Emily, I can't look her in the eyes, I feel so ashamed. If only I had told the truth then."

Nina was right. I couldn't live with myself if I didn't confess. Anyway, no matter what happened, I couldn't possibly feel worse than I already did.

Taking a deep breath, I marched back to Jenn. "I need to talk."

She put an arm around me. "Know something, Remy, I'm glad you got on my case about entering this tournament. You girls put your hearts into the games, and now we've got a good chance of winning first place. Feels good, eh?" Her eyes sparkled with pre-game excitement.

Turns out, I was wrong — I could feel worse.

Rooting my feet in the ground, I forced myself to say, "I did something wrong."

Jenn studied my face for a moment, then called to the rest of the team. "Go to the field and warmup. You know the drill. I'll join you in a minute."

"The red team isn't coming," I blurted. "It's my fault."

By the time I croaked out my confession, I was bawling. And Jenn looked dizzy. She stared into space, ignoring me. Abruptly, she turned and said. "I must talk to Mrs. Jenkins." Without another word, she walked off.

"Sorry," I called after her.

Lame. One little word couldn't fix what I had done.

"The worst is over," Nina said, trying to calm me down. "It'll be okay. You'll see."

Jenn spoke briefly to the convener who was standing by the concession booth. Then she came jogging back.

"What happened?" I asked, afraid of the answer.

Jenn looked me square in the eyes. "Our team is disqualified."

The words felt like a punch. "No! That's not fair to the others. I'm the one who screwed up. I should get punished."

"The decision is final," Jenn said, firmly. "And there's more, Remy — you may not be allowed to play in the league for the rest of the season. The convener is going to meet with the board of directors and decide."

A loud shudder racked my body. The tears I had been holding back broke loose.

"Why don't you go home," Jenn said, putting a hand on my shoulder. "I'll explain to the team."

"B-but, I should …" I couldn't finish my sentence.

"Look, you messed up big-time," Jenn said, "and your team-mates are going to be upset. But it took guts to come to me. I think you should let me handle this now."

"Jenn's right," Nina said, yanking me away. "The team will need time to cool off. I'll even take care of your parents," she promised, glancing over their way. "I'll tell them you need time to chill, and that you'll talk to them later. Okay?"

I nodded sadly and followed her off the field.

Thanks to Nina, my parents didn't interrogate me. But my tear-stained face couldn't lie. It screamed: guilty!

At home, I rushed past Mom, leaving Nina there, and dis-appeared to my bedroom with Tucker. "Your problems are sim-ple compared to mine," I said, snuggling with him. "How am I ever going to face the world?"

He licked my face. No teeth, just tongue. My first kiss! Tucker must have sensed I needed cheering up.

Later, Mom came knocking on my door, a ginger ale in her hand. "Thirsty?"

I shook my head.

She took one small step into my room. "Feel like talking?"

"No," I said, truthfully, "but you're going to find out, and I want you to hear it from me."

Mom gave me a lopsided smile. She sat at the edge of my bed and waited patiently while I found the courage to speak.

"Mom," I warned, "you're going to be disappointed in me."

She tweaked my nose gently. "Let me decide."

Resting my head against Tucker's shoulder, I began to tell Mom the story, in bits and pieces, starting a year ago. When I finished, she squeezed my hand and offered me a sad smile. "Maybe you had to get lost before you could find yourself."

"You're not mad?" I said, confused.

"You are angry enough with yourself, Remy," she said. "But I do have one suggestion: talk to Alison. You need to settle your problems, don't let them grow."

I sat up straight on the bed. "Are you kidding? By now, she will know that I tried to get her team defaulted. She'll never speak to me again."

"That's possible," Mom said. "But you'll never know if you don't try. I'm going to the Andrews' at seven o'clock this evening. As you suspected, they are selling their home, and I need to put up the sign. While I'm there, why don't I see if I can arrange for you and Alison to chat?"

"Good luck," I said, falling back on my bed. "It'll take a miracle."

When Mom left the room, she placed the ginger ale on my night table. The cool beverage helped cool my frazzled head. Sitting there, I replayed the day in my mind. Everything had been going so well, winning both games and advancing to the championship. And then….

Suddenly, I realized there was one mistake I could fix. Reaching across the night table, I picked up the phone and dialed.

"Hey, what's up?" I said, in a soft voice.

"Remy." Lucas made my name sound cold.

"Uh, about today … I won't rat you out. We all make dumb mistakes."

He didn't answer, but I knew he was listening because I could hear him breathing.

"Good luck with the science contest," I said.

He exhaled loudly. "You mean it?"

"Yeah," I said. "With your dedication, one day your experiments will lead to something big."

Lucas must have been totally shocked. All he could say was, "Wow! Thanks!"

When I hung up, I just sat there, thinking. Mom had said something that stuck in my head. Pulling my knees up into my chest, I rocked back and forth. What did she mean when she said I had to get lost before I could find myself?

My thoughts drifted to school, to the rows of "lost and found" boxes, overflowing with clothing and other stuff lost by students. At the end of the year, most of the boxes are still full. How many items get found? How many stay lost forever? Rolling over, I buried my head in the pillow. What were the chances I'd ever find myself?

14

Chocolate Dreams

Mom broke the news during church. "Alison is expecting you after the service."

"What?" My reply came out louder than expected.

"Shhh … the minister is speaking."

Mom had pulled off a miracle.

During the sermon, the minister preached about forgiveness. If only Alison were listening to this, I thought. She might find a way to forgive me. As it was, I'd rated my situation hopeless.

When I got home, I pulled on jean shorts and a T-shirt, then forced down an egg salad sandwich for lunch. Once again, that little voice inside was instructing me to flee. But I knew I had to face up to Alison. No matter how far I ran, she would still be there when I got back. Anyway, I owed her a major apology. But how could I face her? What could I possibly say?

All I knew was that I had to go over. I had to try.

I wheeled my bike out of the garage. As I rode along, pedalling slowly, a weird feeling came over me. I couldn't remember the last time I had travelled this route. The houses seemed strange yet familiar. A few blocks farther along, the temperature suddenly dropped and the wind whipped up. Black clouds gathered overhead. Could it be rain, after a long dry spell?

Approaching the Andrewses house, I noticed the "For Sale"

sign on the lawn. Alison and her brother, Jordan, had been born in that house. I wondered how she felt about moving.

Mrs. Andrews greeted me at the door. "Nice to see you, Remy," she said, with a warm smile. "I know this is hard for you. Alison is waiting in her bedroom. You may go right up."

"Thanks," I mumbled, suddenly wishing I had stayed at home.

In the upstairs hallway, I met Butterscotch. Her nose wiggled as I approached. "Remember me?" I said, bending down to pet her. Startled, she hopped into the bathroom and hid behind the toilet. My heart sank. Butterscotch had forgotten me.

Alison's bedroom door was closed, so I gave a little knock. No answer. I knocked louder.

"Go away!"

Some miracle. Looked like Mom and Mrs. Andrews had cooked up this meeting without Alison's consent.

"Alison," I called through the door, "can we talk?"

"Nothing you can say will change what you did."

"I know … but I want to explain."

The door opened a crack. Her blue eyes drilled through me.

"I'm really sorry," I began, "About everything."

"Time's up." The door slammed in my face.

I took the hint.

At the front door, Mrs. Andrews gave a helpless shrug. "I'm very sorry, Remy."

Outside, rain streaked across my face. My own tears had dried up, leaving me feeling empty. I pedalled hard and fast. At home, I parked my bike in the garage and ran inside.

"That was fast," Mom commented. "How did it go?"

"Alison hates me," I said, burying my face in Tucker's fur. "She didn't want to hear my side."

Mom sighed. "You tried. That's all anyone can do."

"Whatever."

"I have an idea," Mom said, her voice rising. "Let's bake cookies."

Mom ... baking? How long had it been?

When I didn't respond, she dangled the jar of cocoa before my eyes. "Chocolate Dreams," I said, my eyes popping out. "My favourite!"

They used to be Alison's favourite, too.

Dad jogged into the kitchen, tugging up his loose pants. "Did I hear cookies?"

As I mixed the cocoa into the butter and sugar, Dad and Tucker looked on.

"You know," Dad said, "I haven't eaten a Tasty Treat since that night in the garage. Getting caught red-handed made me feel pretty foolish, and it made me think. Sneaking around eating junk food, I wasn't being honest with my family or myself. That night I did some serious thinking. If the doctor is worried about my health, then I should be, too. I made a promise to myself: from now on, I'm going to make better food choices."

"Do Chocolate Dreams fit in your plan?" I asked, spooning blobs onto a cookie sheet.

"Once in a while," he said with a wink.

The phone rang. Nina was calling to ask about my visit with Alison.

"Disaster!" I said, licking batter off my fingers. "Come over. I'll dish you the dirt in person. I'm baking cookies."

"I can't," she said. "My family is going to a pooja this afternoon."

"Excuse me. Pooja?"

She laughed. "A housewarming party. My parents' friends moved to Glendale, and we are welcoming them Indian style."

I heard the doorbell ring. Mom called, "Remy, it's for you." There was something in her voice that ...

I said goodbye to Nina and hurried to the door. On the other side of the screen stood Alison.

"Uh … hey," I said, frozen in my steps.

She closed her umbrella. "Mom made me come. She says I was rude."

"Don't worry about it," I said, waving her off. "I understand why you won't talk to me. It's cool."

I started to close the door, but she pushed back. "Wait, I promised Mom I'd listen."

"Like you said, there's nothing I can say to change things." To be honest, I wanted her to go away. I wanted to return to the kitchen where I felt safe and accepted. But she didn't look like she was going anywhere. Reluctantly, I took her to my bedroom.

Sitting cross-legged on the edge of my bed, Alison gazed around. "Nice bedspread," she said, stroking the fuzzy puppies that had been woven into the fabric. "New?"

I nodded mutely.

We sat in silence, each claiming an end of the bed.

"Go ahead," she said, stone-faced.

Staring at the wall, I mustered up the courage to speak. "Last year when you left for soccer camp in England, you didn't say a word. I showed up at the Glendale soccer camp, waiting for you, and when the instructor told me you had withdrawn, I didn't believe her because, like, I was sure you'd tell me first."

Alison shifted uncomfortably on the bed. She didn't say a word.

"You were gone a whole month and all that time you never sent a postcard or an e-mail. And when you got back, you didn't phone me."

She stared at the bedspread, outlining a puppy's head with her finger. Her silence started to freak me out.

I forced myself to go on. "Remember that day in the washroom when I fell out of the stall?"

She nodded, not looking up.

"I overheard you tell Emily that you had a plan to beat us in the tournament. A couple of days later, Nina sprained her ankle in a freshly dug hole in our practice field."

I expected Alison to defend herself, but she didn't. Strange. She always had something to say.

"At the next practice, we discovered more holes. When Tucker broke loose, you and Emily came running out from behind a hill. You were holding something in your hand. I thought it was a trowel."

What was going on? Why wouldn't she stick up for herself?

Finally, I fired a direct question at her. "What were you two doing?"

At least she looked up at me. "Jenn Rentola is the best coach in the league," she said, quietly. "I figured she'd teach your team some cool plays, so I brought binoculars to spy."

"So that was your plan." I blushed, feeling silly. "On the tournament day I heard you and Emily talking about a secret weapon. That's when I flipped."

"My dad was going to bring Butterscotch, the team mascot," she said under her breath.

The red team's secret weapon — a bunny.

"For whatever it's worth, once I realized I was wrong, I tried to fix things. But it was too late. I am so sorry. I totally get it if you never speak to me again," I told Alison.

She looked up. She was crying. "You must hate me — to think I would do those things."

"That's not it," I said quickly. "My feelings were hurt, but that's no excuse."

"There's something you should know," she said. "Last spring, Mom and Dad began to argue all the time. I used to sit in my bedroom, holding my hands over my ears to block out the yelling."

I leaned toward her side of the bed. "You never said anything."

She shook her head. "Not even to my brother who was in the next room. I kept hoping they would make up. I was afraid if I talked about it, somehow, that would make it real. Then one day, Dad came to me, telling me I was going to soccer camp in England. My parents didn't ask me. They sent me. I thought they were trying to get rid of me — like I was the problem."

I moved a bit closer, closing the gap between us. "If you had only told me."

"I tried," she said, "after I came back. But when I saw you that day at the mall, you wouldn't speak to me. Remember?"

Thinking back, I bit my lip. I had been browsing in the Jean Factory when I backed into her. She gave me a funny smile and said, "Hey."

Angry that she had not even bothered to phone me, I coldly replied, "Do I know you?"

That was the end of our conversation. We both walked away.

But now my eyes reached out to her. "Are you doing okay?"

"I think so," she said. "Now that Dad has moved out, my parents are actually speaking to each other. We're all getting along better."

"What about the move?"

She shrugged. "I don't have a choice, but your mom is helping us find a place close by so that Jordan and I won't have to transfer schools. Mom agrees we've all had enough trauma in our lives."

I swallowed hard. "I know *sorry* won't make a difference."

Her eyes widened. "It can, if you mean it."

"I do," I said, letting out a long sigh. "More than you know."

She gave me a thoughtful look. "Do you think we could be friends again?"

"When I first heard you were moving, I realized that, in my heart, we've always been friends."

She reached out and hugged me. "I missed you, too." Next thing I knew we were both bawling.

"That must have been some camp," I said, when I could speak. "Your game improved a lot. I was so jealous."

She wiped her tears. "Over in England, all I had was football. That poor ball took a lot of hard kicks."

"Brilliant!" I said, putting on an accent.

"That smell," she said, sniffing the air. "Is it Chocolate Dreams?"

My eyes lit up. "Hurry," I said, running for the door, "before Dad eats them all."

When we stormed the kitchen, Mom was bringing the cookies out of the oven.

"Let's eat!" I cried, grabbing a plate.

"They need to cool," Mom warned.

"We like them hot," Alison piped up.

"Tell you what," Mom said, pulling off the oven mitts. "I've got work to do in the garden. Why don't you two finish baking? There is another batch to go in the oven."

Grabbing a spatula, I scooped the cookies onto a plate. Alison grabbed the milk from the fridge and we sat down.

"Mmmm … chocolate," I gurgled, as a warm cookie melted in my mouth.

"These taste totally dreamy," Alison said, holding one in each hand.

Tucker ate the crumbs that fell to the floor. Dad grabbed a small one and went outside to help Mom. When we were alone, Alison and I toasted our new friendship with glasses of milk.

Maybe this time we would get it right.